Straightaway

TURNS IN LOVE SERIES: BOOK THREE

NO MORE LEFT TURNS

RENÉE A. MOSES

GUSSYFLO PUBLISHING

To my great-grandmother, Gustavia. I love you.

Happy Birthday Momma AKA Grandma Bunny! I had to drop this on your day. You keep asking how the story will end lol. I love you and am grateful for your support, honesty, and faith in me.

CHAPTER ONE

Denise

THERE I STOOD, OUTSIDE THE FRONT DOOR OF MY home. Well, what used to be my home. Now, it was merely a house where my so-called husband lived.

What was I doing? Why did I still have a key?

A year ago, when my world proved to be fake, I distinctly remember leaving all of my keys in a drawer in the kitchen. But the same set was about to assist me with re-entering the crime scene of the death of my trust. My love. My marriage.

With a turn of the inserted key and a push of the twisted doorknob, soft moans echoed into the foyer. The male groaning was undoubtedly my husband. I didn't recognize the woman. How would I?

At that moment, my feet should have guided me back over the threshold I crossed a second ago. However, curiosity dragged me toward the noises.

My husband was fucking another woman *again*.

Yeah, I left over a year ago. We spoke very little in that time, but he could've told me he had moved on. We weren't even divorced yet. Not one time had we discussed it as a finality.

Each step reset my pulse as if I took off in a hundred-yard dash. The closer I got to the master bedroom door, the louder they became.

I counted to three to prepare myself for whatever my eyes would witness. Then I forced the door wide open to find Brian in bed with Kim.

They didn't stop. I didn't stop watching. It hit me that he loved her more than he ever loved me.

My eyes moistened until a tear dropped. As soon as it rolled to my chin, a loud burst came from the front door.

My cousin, Bam, ran in my direction with a gun in each hand. I backed away when she passed me screaming and cursing at them.

A gunshot went off.

"Dee! Dee! Wake up, girl." Momma shook my shoulder, pulling me from my nap. I cracked one eye open.

"Girl, get up. I need to head to work. Your dad is out for the afternoon. Come get Layla so I can go," she told me.

"Okay." I slowly sat up and stretched my arms as far as they could go. My back cracked a few times since I fell asleep slouched over.

The last thing I remembered before closing my eyes was managing the inbox for a client of mine. Teressa Jennings was an influencer, author, speaker, and now an online teacher. She had an excess of email inquiries from her eager students and wanted genuine communication with them. Teressa hated auto- responders which put money in my pocket.

Being a virtual assistant to a few busy professionals kept me occupied. After being with my parents, who wouldn't take rent money from their broken-hearted daughter, I saved most of it. I'd soon use it to find my own place.

I walked into the living room where Layla pressed random buttons on her read-aloud book in the playpen.

"You are working a lot lately," Momma stated, pouring a cup of coffee.

"I have to, so we can get on our feet."

She looked up, but her gaze was on the wall of cabinets in front of her. "Baby, you don't have to do this alone. Your husband wants to take care of you. Why won't you let him? He's sorry. Let him do his job."

"His job is to love his daughter and make sure she's good. Even I cannot deny that he does that astonishingly well. Especially since no one asked me what I wanted."

"Oh, don't go there again. Your father did the right thing by letting Brian see Layla. He did not betray your trust like you whined about before. You were being hard-headed. Someone had to step up. Who else other than your dad? Family comes first with him always."

"Brian is *not* his family." I crossed my arms over my chest feeling justified. Everyone treated Brian like he belonged where he didn't.

"No, but he *is* Layla's." She made a face as if she proved a point.

"It doesn't matter anymore."

"You're right. It doesn't."

Momma sat down at the bar with me to drink her almost black coffee. It contained a pinch of sugar, no cream. How could she stand the taste?

"Now, back to the real topic. Why are you being so stubborn with Brian? That man is here every chance he gets trying to win his family back. You act like you found out he was a pimp or some kingpin behind your back."

"But—"

Momma raised her hand to shut me up. "He messed up. We get it. He knows it. It was a one-time indiscretion. What will it take for you to forgive him? Brian is a good man."

"He's not good enough. The man I thought I knew would

have never let me down the way he did. Brian not only stabbed me in the back, he stabbed me in the heart. The knife is still there. So, no! I cannot go back to him. Ever!"

"Dee? Come on, baby. It's not the end of all things. You can get through this with him. I believe it."

"Momma, I can't even sleep in peace. I keep dreaming about him and that *girl* in bed. I walk in, and no one cares. It's too much."

"Maybe you can go to therapy with him. A marriage counselor can do wonders. Trust me."

"Nah, I'll just have Bam handle it like she does in my dream."

"Lord, I don't even want to know what that means." She laughed because she understood that anything involving Bam meant someone would get hurt.

"Anyway, why are you going to work on a Saturday afternoon?"

"My boss lost his thumb drive that had a few reports I completed this week. Since he's out of town, he needs me to go to the office and email them. Mr. Cook is so old school. Even at my age, I'm hip to the cloud. But he doesn't want his work to become vulnerable to hackers. Nobody cares about his business enough to do any of the mess he fears."

I chuckled at the image of his paranoia.

"Mama! Mama!" Layla squealed when she noticed me.

"Hey, Mommy's little bug." I walked to the playpen and lifted her out.

Layla gave me a big kiss emphasizing the sound as she always did. "Mua!"

"When did she eat last?" I asked Momma who placed her empty cup in the sink.

"Less than an hour ago, but it was a snack. She didn't have a real lunch yet."

"Okay. Thanks for everything."

"Oh girl, please. I would do anything for my girls. Even push that big red button that says 'Don't bring up Brian.'"

I rolled my eyes. "Yeah, you do that too often."

"It's only out of love. And being right," she said, cracking a smile.

"Mmmhmm. Where's Nana?"

"Out in the garden. Well, the outline of a garden. She's getting her list together of what she wants to plant so we can get it going for her."

"That will be nice. I cannot wait to help her harvest the veggies. There's nothing like growing your own food."

"You ain't gonna be here that long. Your butt will be back in Houston where you belong." She winked and picked up her purse.

"I see I've worn out my welcome."

"No. That's not what I'm saying." Momma grabbed at Layla's hand. "Grandma is only trying to make sure the sweetest little baby has both of her parents in her life full-time. That's all. Wouldn't you like that my little snookums?" she asked Layla.

"You won't stop, huh?"

"Can't stop, won't stop," she sang, doing some lame dance move.

"Don't hurt yourself, *Grandma*?"

"Hey, watch how you say it. I'm not old. I still got moves."

"Yeah, sure you do, Momma."

Her phone buzzed on the counter. When she looked at the notification, she rolled her eyes. "Lemme get out of here before this man drive me nuts."

"Alright. Love you!"

"Love you more."

Momma kissed my cheek and pretended to eat Layla's hand. My bug loved that. She giggled until her grandma stopped and exited through the garage door.

ᴘᴘᴘ

THE FOLLOWING SATURDAY, I checked out a few apartments near my parents' neighborhood. My dad took Layla to visit Brian wherever they met. The secret was out, but I still didn't want to see him.

After more than a year apart, my feelings confused me like crazy. Sometimes I missed my husband and other times I wanted to punch him in the throat or worse.

My dreams didn't help either. There were nights filled with horrible scenes of Brian being with ol' girl or a random woman. Other ones, we're happy together as if nothing ever happened. Dammit, if I didn't wish the latter could be real.

I wanted my old life with a trustworthy best friend and husband. Blissfully ignorant to what went on between them. Even if forgiveness proved possible, my memory wouldn't let the thought of them together go.

No one had my back the way I wanted them to. Some days, my family should stick to saying what I wanted to hear. Tell me I could take all the time in the world, or I didn't have to deal with Brian ever. Who cared if it wasn't true?

The initial emotional support had worn off. Before, everyone shared my anger. Now, they pushed me to fix something I did not break.

"Do it for Layla," they'd say.

Brian didn't. He screwed over the both of us while Layla dwelled in my womb. That reality messed with me daily. Getting over it wasn't as easy as they made it sound.

The only person who experienced my pain shot her cheating husband in the foot. Aunt Rita got away with it. My luck would have my ass in jail.

Layla was the spitting image of her dad. I couldn't avoid him no matter how hard I tried.

When I left the third apartment's office, I received a text

from my mom to see if I'd be home for lunch. She wanted to prepare enough food for me. After learning lunch included crab cakes, I placed my order for about five.

One thing for sure, I gained weight eating all the southern perfection my mom created in the kitchen. Every other Saturday, she'd fry something. We didn't eat healthy all the time, but she did cut back on the fried foods after my grandmother recovered from her health issues.

Aunt Rita pulled into the driveway right behind me. I waited on her to get out of the car so we could walk to the door together.

"You're here for the food?"

"Girl, Patti mentioned them crab cakes on the phone. I hung up and headed over."

We laughed as I opened the door. The smell hit me so hard, I closed my eyes imagining the taste. We sang about what Aunt Rita called "crack cakes." Momma hated how it sounded, but those suckers were addictive.

Momma was in the kitchen frying away, and Nana sat at the table nibbling on her cake. I gave her a kiss and asked for a bite.

"Hell, no. Get yo' own," she playfully snapped.

"Ha! Those crack cakes got Momma ready to fight," Aunt Rita said before kissing Nana's cheek. "How you feeling, honey?"

"I'm just fine. I'd be better if y'all would let me eat in peace. Coming in here with all that noise," Nana complained.

Momma and my aunt gave each other the same look. That meant Nana was in one of her moods.

There were only about six crab cakes done. Momma made sure we took one at a time. The bowl with the mixture had plenty to go around once cooked, so we obeyed. She also had salad in the fridge and mashed potatoes on the counter.

"What were you up to this morning?" Momma asked me.

"Probably the gym," Aunt Rita answered.

Nobody was talking to her, but I wouldn't dare say that aloud. She was the only one who spoke about the weight. It was maybe around fifteen pounds evenly spread. Nothing I couldn't drop without decent effort.

"I'll go when you go." I nudged her. "The apartments I told you about had some units available next month."

"Wait! You were serious?" Momma asked.

"Yes!"

Aunt Rita squinted. "What y'all talking about?"

I swallowed a mouthful of my crab cake. "I want to get my own place."

"She *needs* to make sure it's the right move first," my mom said.

"What's the big deal? We've been separated this long. It's safe to say it's over."

Aunt Rita brought the fork down from her lips. "Maybe for you, but have you talked with Brian about this?"

"Exactly my point," Momma chimed. "She's making this decision as if they're divorced. She won't even talk to the man and now this!"

My mom was getting too worked up over something that wasn't her choice to make. It annoyed me how fighting for this lost cause of a marriage was the only option in their minds.

"Here comes the prettiest little girl on the planet," Dad sang, walking through the front door. Layla ran inside the house.

My dad looked dead into my eyes while holding the door open after he stepped inside.

"Look who's here," he announced.

Brian walked in with his hands in his jean's front pockets and had that stupid half-smile on his face. His nervous expression never changed, and I was already convinced that neither would he. So, what the hell was he doing here?

CHAPTER TWO

Brian

I HADN'T LAID EYES ON MY WIFE IN OVER A YEAR. One mistake cost me everything. No time soon would I give up on getting my family back.

The first step was to talk to Denise. My father-in-law, Stan, made a part of that happen by allowing me into his home. The rest fell on me.

Denise's glare burned a hole through my chest. It hurt. Her nose flaring, as if she'd snap at any second, sent chills up my spine.

"Hi, everyone." I waved at the women.

"Dad? Come on!" she almost yelled.

"Dee, please? I made—"

She turned her neck so fast to shut me up. I did.

"Pumpkin, you are adults who made a vow before God. And you are parents. The least you can do after all this time is talk to your husband."

Denise scoffed. "We have nothing to discuss. He made that very clear when he—"

"Please?" I walked closer to where everyone gathered near the kitchen table. Layla rushed to me, and I picked her up.

9

Once she lay her head on my shoulder, Denise's scowl softened.

"I have nothing to say to you," she said looking down at the kitchen table.

Wrapping my other arm around Layla to secure her, I stepped closer. "You don't have to say anything. I'll talk. Please, Dee?"

"Stop calling me that."

I nodded in obedience. "Okay. Can we go outside for a minute?"

Patti met Denise's glare before tilting her head. My estranged wife rolled her eyes and released the longest breath before looking my way.

"One minute. And I *mean* one."

More time would be better, but I'd take what I could get at this point. Stan threw me a confident smirk before taking Layla.

"You got this, son," he cheered under his breath. With a quick nod, I opened the front door for Denise. She smacked her lips at my gesture. This may be the hardest minute of my life.

Once on the porch, Denise sat on a white, worn rocking bench. When I moved to sit beside her, she shot a glare that cursed me out in every language. So, I leaned against the post in front of her.

The anger on her face and even in her posture was something I hadn't experienced in all the years I'd known her. We didn't have a perfect marriage nor a tumultuous one. Our spats were minimal and caused by attitudes after a stressful day. Maybe we were fooling ourselves and not being true to who we were.

I never raised my voice at her because my mother taught me not to. Denise didn't either. The arguments we had were short-lived and resolved with a conversation. It was like that every single time. Neither of us was ever pushed to the edge where we'd lose it. Until now.

My wife sat there avoiding any connection. "Your minute is running down," she barked, observing the people in the park nearly right across the street.

"Oh, um...Denise, I understand that you still hate me for what I did and I can't blame you."

She sucked her teeth.

I moved to block her view of the park so she could see me. She turned the other direction.

"Dee, please look at me."

"I don't want to. And I told you not to call me that."

"How can I apologize if you won't even hear me out?"

Denise stared into my eyes. "You can apologize until the day you die, and it won't change anything."

"It will still be worth it," I said, resting on my knees.

She folded her arms across her chest. "What?"

"If I have to tell you how sorry I am and how much I love you until I die, it's worth it. You are my life. For some stupid reason, I lost track of it one time. Then shit went all over the place and was beyond my control. I made a mistake. I live it every second of every day. You and Layla are everything. I will spend all of my days proving that to you. Please give me a chance to—"

"Times up. If that is all, I need to get back inside."

Denise hopped from the rocking bench and brushed off the back of her pants.

I popped up and caught her hand. She pulled away and killed me again with those eyes. "Denise, please? I am begging you to let me back in. Even if I have to move here, I will do it."

Her eyes widened before she finally made eye contact that felt familiar. No scowl, no hardness, just my wife.

"Why would you move here?"

"To be closer to you. To be closer to Layla. I cannot do this much longer, Denise."

"Then don't. Leave us alone and be where you truly want to be. We both know where that is. Or should I say with whom?"

"Yeah, you can say that. Because I am standing in front of the same person you're talking about."

Her lips raised to the side like they always did when skeptical. I moved a little closer, and she didn't back away. "This is where I want to be. Wherever my wife and daughter are. There is no other way to live."

"I do not trust your word, Brian. I don't trust you."

"That's fair, but I can prove that you can trust me again. If you let me."

She said nothing. I took that as an opening. "Say the word. Tell me you'd at least let me try. I will pack up everything and stay here with you."

"You can't stay here," she snapped, pointing to the front door.

"Not literally right here. I mean nearby. I'd get a place here so that I can be close to my family."

"What about your family back home?"

"You are the only family that matters, Denise. You two are my life, *my* family."

"Mm."

"Look, I know it's not an easy decision for you considering the mess I made. Think about it. Tell me what I can do to make this right. Whatever you say, I *will* do it."

I wanted to hold her so bad, but she'd close up. This was the first time in a year that she listened to what I had to say. Her not bringing up the minute after the second time was a huge deal.

Denise had been snappy as hell, understandably. I could never get a word in, and she wouldn't say more than a few.

Stan and Patti were a big reason I was bold enough to come here today. Oddly, they'd forgiven me and encouraged me to try harder after I convinced myself that all was lost.

"I don't know, Brian."

Her response gave me hope. It could've been her normal "hell no." Uncertainty could go either way and proved that there may be a possibility. I'd take that.

"Okay. I understand."

She turned toward the door. "Dee, do you mind if I say goodbye to Layla?"

Denise shook her head and left the door open for me. When Stan looked my way, I shrugged. Layla sat in her high-chair with cheese crackers and a sippy cup.

Patti took Layla out so that I could give her a hug. After a few words, I put my baby down.

"You're on your way out?" Denise's aunt asked.

"Yes, ma'am. I have to be at the airport in a few hours."

"Well, what are you going to do until then?" Patti asked.

Denise's head whipped toward her mother. "Momma, don't!"

"Oh, hush up. He is still my son-in-law. I can talk to him."

All eyes landed on me. I glanced at Denise, who sat back in her chair with her hand on her forehead.

"Sorry about your rude wife. So, do you have any plans until your flight?" Patti continued.

"No, ma'am. I'm gonna grab some food from somewhere and eat at the room."

"So, how far is it this time? It can't be an hour away like before," she asked.

"Um, it's only about fifteen minutes."

"Momma, seriously?"

Patti gave her daughter a stern face that she'd clearly developed first. It was one that Denise wore whenever irritated. My wife left the room.

"I should get going. I think I've caused enough trouble."

"Nonsense! We've talked plenty about all of this already. Have we not?" Patti asked.

Ms. Rita sat in silence, but her eyes followed us each time we spoke.

"We have. But she isn't ready for me to be around and I need to respect that."

Patti sucked her teeth. "Even though you screwed up monumentally, you are a good man. I believe you will do right by our daughter from now on."

"Yes, ma'am. I only have to convince her."

Stan rose from his seat in the living room, passing me to get to the kitchen. "You will, son." He squeezed my shoulder on his way.

"Well, let me make you a to-go plate. I know we made it awkward enough." Patti giggled. "Denise will come around."

"I hope so." I smiled at the sight of my mother-in- law rinsing a styrofoam container she got from a stack in her pantry.

She had the same setup in her house before they moved here. We ate at their place most Sundays. Patti used to say she never received her good storage containers back and having the styrofoam ones fixed the problem.

After stuffing crab cakes and sides into the container, she wrapped the entire thing in foil before tying it inside two plastic bags.

"You want to take a few beers?" Stan asked.

"No, thanks."

All I could think about was Denise in that back room by herself. Her family welcomed me while she wanted nothing to do with me. I wished I could go back there and comfort her, but that would be the last thing she'd want. Mainly since I was the "thing" she needed comfort for.

One last goodbye and I walked out.

At the hotel, I savored every bit of the home-cooked meal. I missed Patti's food. My mom used to rave about these crab cakes. I scarfed them down so fast, I got hiccups.

Mom called to check in. I updated her on the details of my conversation with my wife and even teased her about the food. My flight would get me home in time for my grandmother's surprise birthday party tonight. My mom would pick me up from the airport and head straight there.

Our families meshed well together and our mothers grew into good friends. Many times, the two of them spoke on the phone with my indiscretions as their topic of discussion. Other times, they plotted on how they'd fix my screw up. Today was one of their ideas.

I only got on board with it an hour before I stepped to her parents' front door. Denise wasn't supposed to know that her mother put me up to it. Not that it was a secret that they wanted to see us back together. I assumed my communication with her family might feel like more betrayal. I'd keep that part to myself.

CHAPTER
THREE

Evan locked eyes with me. "What?" I asked because he stared like he'd dozed off with opened eyes.

"Hm?"

"Why you keep looking at me like that?"

He grinned. "Daydreaming."

"About what?"

"You. Us."

Ava hit his coffee table with a toy and scared the hell out of me. Evan burst into laughter at my attempt to jump out of my skin.

Tonight was the third time we'd been at his place this week. It became such a habit that he asked if I wanted a key. I accepted it only because he offered. Anytime we came over, he was home, or the three of us came in together. That was last month, and it changed things for me.

Evan trusted me enough to give me a key. He was also trustworthy, but the comfort of having access put me more at ease.

After many months spending time with each other or as

our little threesome, I fell harder than I expected. Our relationship began when Ava turned one, and now she was almost two. She loved him already.

He didn't seem real at first. A young, black pediatrician with no children approaching me at an appointment for my daughter turned into something I found hard to accept. Evan loved me like nothing I'd ever experienced. The way he got lost in my eyes gave him control. Power that had my ass dazed every time our eyes met until I broke myself away.

Even the smallest touch felt like a closed circuit finally allowing electricity to flow and wake up all its elements. He did that to me. Every sexual element in my body came to life around him.

I'd been attracted to men, naturally, but never pulled toward one like this. No one ever had my ass mesmerized. I always thought it was a bullshit way to sell the whole soul mate nonsense. I didn't know anymore.

If not by his gaze, it was his voice. He had a velvety tenor tone that could talk my panties off. It wasn't crazy deep unless we were in bed. His pillow talk served as foreplay for real. It didn't matter the subject. Listening to his voice tingled my insides.

Plus, the man could sing. Luckily he didn't do it in public. It was bad enough his ass looked like a model or movie star material with a body that took lots of discipline to maintain and smooth, blemish-free milk chocolate skin. That voice would have me fighting chicks off daily.

Evan's heart proved to make this perfect guy unreal. I always thought it was too good to be true for a man with his looks, his heart, values, mind, and lifestyle to be interested in me. A single mom with a turnoff type of backstory regarding Ava's father. Despite everything I came with, Evan loved me still.

We took things slowly, but two months ago we professed our love for one another. We were in month seven, and the other shoe hadn't dropped yet. I became more convinced that there wasn't one.

My punishment for my beyond stupid decisions and mistakes weren't showing up in our relationship. It had to come in some form though. Nothing goes without consequence.

I gained the perfect man and father figure for Ava when Brian wasn't around. How? Why? I didn't deserve him. I didn't deserve the love and passion in his eyes when we were together or the excitement he had whenever he interacted with Ava. They loved each other like family in such a short time. I couldn't understand it enough to enjoy the bliss I should be in. Yes, I was happy, but I feared it wouldn't last long.

I lost my best friend because of one night with the wrong man. My mom still wouldn't look me in the eye for that same mistaken night. I had to start a new career as a freelance writer which wasn't so bad but I missed my old one and my old boss. Everyone I spent my life with before Ava was now thousands of miles away. Maybe these were my consequences.

Evan waved his hand in front of my face. "Babe?"

"Yeah."

"I said do you want me to go get some food. I couldn't make it to the store earlier."

"Oh, uh, I don't care. We can go now if you want."

"Yeah, we can do that." He did it again. The staring. "Damn, you're beautiful."

Just like clockwork, the tingles started in my belly, then shot up and down my body.

"You always say that." I tried my hardest not to blush.

"Because it's true."

"If you say so."

Evan pulled me up and sat me on his lap. Attempting to

hypnotize me with those deep brown eyes, he paused as if trying to find the right words. "I wish you could see what I see when I look at you."

I hid my face in his shoulder. Evan's ways were something to get used to. No one ever said shit like that to me.

Trent was always on ten, so I had to be too. Being always prepared for a fight chipped away the softness that Evan reminded me about myself. He was careful with me, and I still didn't know how to react to him.

All those years with Trent taught me to be hard on myself. Even watching how Brian treated Denise used to make me jealous. Trent let me know he loved my body when he wanted to be inside it. Evan, however, told me what he thought of me every chance he got, and it was never negative.

My eyes were opened to another breed of men that I missed out on. All because of being voluntarily stuck in my screwed up relationship with Trent.

Evan lifted the shoulder that my head rested on and forced me to look at him. "You know I love you, right?"

"Yes. I love you too."

"Then please stop fighting me when I tell you how beautiful you are. Just accept it because it's true."

"Okay."

After a slow kiss, we got Ava together and went to the store. We could fool a stranger that we were a real family. He was mine, and I was his. Evan made me proud to belong to him. I could see us being together for a while. As long as nothing stupid happens. I had a track record for dumb shit blocking me from happiness.

Back at his place, we cooked breakfast for dinner. I had bacon, biscuits, and oatmeal duty. Evan made spinach and mushroom omelets with provolone cheese. Another thing to love. The man could cook better than me, and he loved to do it. That shoe had to drop before I fall too deep and end up hurt.

When we finished eating, I gave Ava a bath and laid her in the toddler bed that Evan put in his second bedroom. It's been there for at least a couple of months. I didn't want to keep leaving Ava with Aunt Viv every time he wanted to see me, so he told me to bring Ava along.

"Kim, come sit with me." He patted the seat on the couch next to him when I walked into the living room. I snuggled under his arm.

"You thought about what I asked you?"

I hoped he wouldn't remember I never got back to him about it. "Evan, we can't move in with you."

"Why not?"

"It's too soon. Don't you think? We haven't even been together a year. I come with a lot of…I don't know. We can't."

"You want to keep driving an hour back and forth to see each other. You always complain about it. I thought this would be a good thing."

I faced him. "I don't want to live with a man who isn't my husband. I'm not saying I am ready for marriage or anything, but shacking up won't work for me. Hell, my grandmother would probably kill both of us. Plus, I have Ava to think about."

"Like she won't mind not having to sit in the car seat for the long drive. I bet if I asked her, she'd say yes." He chuckled. "But I get it. I don't mean to put pressure on you. It's just for the first time in a long ass time, I know what I want, and that's being with you as much as possible. I guess I gotta put a ring on that pretty finger to get you over here."

"Uh, not now you don't." We laughed. "You ain't ready. You still be trippin' about Brian."

He rolled his eyes and shifted in his seat. "That's because he's in love with you."

"Oh my gosh, Evan! No, he isn't. I know it's a crazy situation with him and Ava, but we are not like that."

"Babe, trust me. *I* am in love with you, so I know. The way he acts whenever I'm around, he wants you."

"Brian is Ava's dad. That's all. He is still married and is trying to get Denise back. That's who he loves, and I pray she can forgive what we did and take him back."

"Shit, me too. Then he won't be looking at me sideways like I don't belong. He will have to learn his place because I swear that dude is territorial with you."

"He is only a tad bit jealous that you get so much time with Ava. It's not about me and him. He's not getting the full dad experience he wants."

"If you say so. I know better but I'ma let you think that."

"Shut up." I playfully punched him in the arm.

"Make me." He was at it again with those damn eyes. When his tongue swiped his bottom lip before he bit it, he had me.

Aunt Vivica playfully fussed at me for hooking her up with one of Evan's colleagues. I convinced her to go out on a date after so many years alone. She was only in her fifties and had plenty more years ahead of her. No one would ever replace Uncle Terrell in her heart, but I wanted her to find someone special.

Apparently, Dr. Howard bored her to death. One of these days, I'd find her someone worth her time or maybe he'd find her. Aunt Viv lived alone for years before I came along, but with so much time at Evan's, I felt like I was leaving her behind. She didn't see it that way, but I would still follow through on my mission to get her back to that special happy. That Evan type of happy.

"Anyway, enough about my dry date. What's going on with you and Mr. Right?"

I was in the kitchen making a sandwich for me and mac and cheese for Ava. "What?"

"Oh please, you know what I'm talking about." She got up from the bar stool and grabbed Ava from the playpen. I removed the table part of Ava's highchair to help Aunt Viv out. Ava whined. She acted like she was too big to sit in it. The last time I tried to let her sit at the regular table, her little butt fell.

"Evan is pretty much perfect, but I don't know if he's the one." After spooning the mac and cheese on a kiddie plate, I added some peas and carrots that I warmed up from yesterday. My baby girl usually made a mess, but she loved being able to feed herself. I gladly cleaned the mess. She looked so cute.

"The hell! I know true love from experience and the way that man looks at you and you at him, it's the real thing."

"It's too soon for all that, Auntie. I ain't gon' lie and say I don't love him, but I have Ava, and I'm trying to get myself together before—"

"Before what? A fine ass man sweeps you off your feet? It's a little late for that. You better stop being all hard and let him in."

"You getting' all fired up and cussin'. I guess that means I should listen."

We laughed at her newfound attitude. "Excuse me, angel. Your momma keeps upsetting me," she said to Ava.

"Whatever. You know what I come with is a lot to ask someone to accept. Once he sees the whole picture, he might run away."

"Haven't you told him everything?"

"Yes, but—"

"But nothing. Stop being hard-headed."

"My mom is a mess, and you know it. She might scare him off. Then his past causes him to be suspicious of everything regarding Brian. He gets all bothered about him."

"Okay, but that's minor stuff. If Diana can cause him to run, then *he's* crazy. But with Brian, maybe you should have them talk it out. If Evan is seriously in love with you, he will need to face the man he's threatened by. Brian is a sweetheart. Evan will see that nothing is going on."

A meeting between those two? Why didn't I think of that?

CHAPTER FOUR

Denise

Moving day was around the corner, and I had a few errands to run. I owned nothing to furnish an apartment. This morning, I left Layla with her grandmother. Debbie wouldn't let me get away with living in a hotel for two weeks. She lived in Stafford, which was close enough to my new abode, and everywhere I needed to go today.

In the past month, I'd been all over the place. If someone said I'd move back to Houston, I would've laughed in their face. Hell, I did whenever my parents suggested this move instead of staying in Atlanta.

Brian's visit changed my perspective, and I finally put Layla at the forefront. The way she loved her dad flew over my head this whole time. I'd never seen them together since I left. My father snuck Layla off so much that she developed a bond with Brian.

When she ran to her father at my parents' house, it reminded me that I had to be mature and do right by my daughter. That did not mean we'd get back together. Only that she deserved closeness with her dad.

Momma wouldn't let me allow Brian to move to Georgia

since he'd have to find another job, sell the house, and whatever else. He deserved to drop and rearrange everything but as my mother said, I shouldn't be spiteful. The move would be easier for me since I could work from anywhere.

I swore up and down I'd do whatever I could to make a good life for Layla. Moving back to Houston was a step I had to take to keep my promise.

Before settling in on this decision, Brian texted me daily. At first, he sent all apology messages and appreciation for hearing him out. Then they turned into sweet ones about missing his family and wanting to spend more time with Layla and me.

My eyes rolled constantly. The messages turned into longer ones and sometimes love memes or even songs. He did a lot of the same things when we first fell in love. Some of those feelings crept back in, but I stomped them out.

Brian was always a decent man. He took pride in being honest and slow to anger. He practiced admirable patience. We had a few hiccups now and then but never anything that caused us to walk away. I loved him more than life because of how he treated me.

What he did ripped my soul to pieces because it wasn't like him. Not the man I'd grown to love and cherish. Not the man I spent all of my days with. It didn't seem feasible, yet it happened.

My husband became simply a man. To me, he was better than all of them. He had more respect, honor, and pride in being a good person. Damn near an angel. Then he revealed his broken wings. He showed me he wasn't so perfect. It killed me. It killed the image of this amazing guy on this pedestal because I believed he belonged there.

Over time, I grasped that Brian made a mistake he assured he wouldn't repeat. Trusting him to pull it off was a different story. A year and some change later, I still lacked faith in him.

Momma told me I could never trust him again if I didn't give him an opportunity to prove himself. The thought of going back seemed too risky. Did I want to get sucked into his world only to end up back here? Back in this internal fight where I blamed myself for ever giving him all of me. I knew better but being in it made my mind explore the most ridiculous possibilities of why. Why me? Why would he do this? What did *I* do wrong?

Aunt Rita constantly bashed her ex-husband but had a soft spot for Brian. She'd say, "Sometimes people do stuff they don't mean. They screw up and have idiotic moments. Your husband is the type of person that had the odds already stacked against him to do stupid shit. Why? Because he's a man."

She believed with everything in her that men were about the dumbest creatures on the planet. And even worse when it came to relationships. They didn't always think things through and could be compulsive in the worst situations. To her, Brian was a victim of thinking with the wrong head one time.

Her logic was bullshit. Men could be as supportive and thoughtful and faithful as anyone else. They were in control of their actions the same as we were.

With temptation, there were two choices. Unfortunately, my husband bailed on his vows. No different than if some man threw himself at me. I could screw him or remember that I had a husband at home. It was that simple.

Everyone shared what they felt I should do for so long. I only recently considered their opinions. I couldn't understand them pushing for me to run back in the arms of a cheater. Then I realized that my family would never steer me into something they felt would hurt me. They truly believed that Brian had a "fuck up" moment that wouldn't repeat itself.

For my father to be so gung-ho about our reconciliation, I

had to weigh my options. My dad was the ultimate protector, especially of me. And there he was trying to fix my marriage. His pushes did it for me. He'd never tell me to go back if he felt I'd be in harm's way emotionally or in any other case. So, here I was moving back home to find out if they were right.

I signed a six-month lease for an apartment in Stafford. A two-bedroom went for a lot more than I thought. Still cheaper than the ones near my parents' neighborhood. I wanted to rent a house, but they were tripping with those prices. I could've had an office and guest room. Oh well.

Debbie kept in contact with me since I left Houston, but it felt distant. We spent a lot of time together before this foolishness. She wasn't a smothering mother-in-law, and I loved that about her. Our relationship started as family by association even before I married her son. About two years into datingBrian, Debbie and I considered each other a friend.

So, living with her for the past week put me back in a comfort zone. We talked briefly about her son and not one time did she defend his actions. She was extremely disappointed in the situation but had no choice other than acceptance. I had a choice.

Debbie mentioned Brian's other daughter, Ava, so much that I asked her to stop. It wasn't the baby's fault. I wasn't at a place where I could discuss her or listen to anything regarding her. Since Debbie boasted about her granddaughters verbally, her home did the same.

When I first arrived, I had a brief thought to take my ass to a hotel. The house threw Ava all in my face from every angle. Layla was on the walls, bookshelves, and tables, too.

Debbie had pictures I took with my baby. She said my momma sent them. I hadn't seen most of the other ones. They captured her growth over the past year. Many were professional photos with Brian.

A few months ago, my dad told me about Brian's visits,

but I didn't know they did all of this. Even when I spoke to Debbie on the phone, she never mentioned seeing Layla on video calls whenever Brian came to Atlanta.

I didn't find out until last month when I apologized for keeping Layla from her. She was sympathetic to my state of mind and assured me that all wasn't lost.

During the worst time in my life, I kept Layla to myself to make a point. I wanted Brian to know that he'd miss out on his daughter because of his choices. I only recently regretted that part. My anger had my nose in the air, and my baby could have suffered for it.

Because of my father's will to do the right thing even against my wishes, my daughter still knew her dad and grandmother. I was grateful he went behind my back. There was no way I would've allowed it. Only now did I understand the importance of separating my feelings so Layla could have the family she deserved. She needed the people that loved her the most, which included her dad.

For every image of my baby, another one hung of Brian's other child. It made me sick to my stomach, but I had to be an adult. While I couldn't avoid the pictures, I could ask to not talk about Ava. Debbie agreed for the time being.

How could my mother-in-law not love her grandchildren? It was a lot to ask of her, so I made a note to get out of her house more. I didn't want her to be uncomfortable on my account.

After going to three furniture stores, browsing at IKEA, and having lunch with an old church friend, I finally made it back to Debbie's place. Brian's car sat in the driveway. I would've pulled off, but someone looked through the blinds from the front window and caught me. From the height of the opening, it was him.

I sat in the car for a few minutes to gather my thoughts and remind myself that this was the right decision. Even if I left, there was nowhere to go and no telling how long he planned on staying.

Be an adult.

"Mama!" Layla squealed, eyes big. She ran to me, and I picked her up, giving her the longest hug. I'd never left her with anyone but my family. She was still in one piece and wore a smile that gave me butterflies.

Brian stood up. "Hey, Denise."

"Hey." I gave him a quick glance.

"How was your day?" he asked.

I put Layla down. "Good."

Debbie walked into the living room. "Girl, you had a long day. You want me to make you a plate? I just finished."

"No, thank you. I had a big lunch."

"Oh, good. I don't know why I thought you didn't eat all this time." She chuckled to herself.

"Um, I need to get Layla bathed and ready for bed."

Brian scrunched his face and rocked his head. Debbie must've noticed it. "Your wife—"

My eyes darted her way.

"Oh, uh, Denise likes to take Layla baths early," she explained to her son.

I let Layla take one more drink of her apple juice before leaving the room to get her ready. I heard Brian and his mother speaking, but I didn't care to make out what they were talking about.

With our suitcases still packed, I had to dig through one to find pajamas for the night. Even after doing laundry yesterday, I folded and placed everything back into the suitcase, ready to leave at any time.

In the bathroom, Layla tried to undress herself. As she struggled, I ran her bath before helping her. She flashed all of her little teeth once her head came through her shirt.

"Dada!" she said before dancing around. I couldn't hold back my smile. She'd break out into a dance anywhere.

My focus attended the water to make sure it didn't get too hot or too high. Then came Layla's favorite part—bubbles. I saw Brian in the mirror standing in the doorway watching me, but I didn't turn around.

"Hey, um, do you mind if I help?"

"You don't have to. It's not much to do."

He cleared his throat. "Yeah, I know. I hadn't had the chance to give our daughter a bath. I could help."

Releasing air through my nostrils only, I nodded. "If you want to, Brian."

"Are you still mad at me?" He walked all the way inside to get Layla's bottoms off.

I kept my hand in the tub to monitor the temperature. "Can we not do this now? We are here so Layla can be closer to you."

"What about you?"

"What about me?"

"Do you want to get closer again? Like, try to work things out?"

I told him to put Layla on the toilet to see if she'd use it before her bath.

"She's potty trained already?"

"No, I recently introduced it to her. She only peed in it once. Starting early."

"Cool," he said before letting her go. I hurried and caught her before she fell into the damn toilet. "Shit! I mean...I'm sorry. I assumed she could sit on it."

"Nope, she's too small. You have to hold her."

"My bad, Layla. Daddy doesn't have much experience taking care of you yet."

"Who's fault is that?" I mumbled.

Brian backed away. When Layla let nothing out, I put her

in the tub and sat on the edge.

"I guess that answered my question."

"Can you watch her?"

"Of course."

"Stay close in case she falls back or anything."

In the room we stayed in, I sat on the bed and inhaled as much air as I could before slowly releasing it. Keeping up with an attitude was easier when we were hundreds of miles apart. Seeing his face, feeling his energy, hearing his voice. It became overwhelming already.

Back in the bathroom, I grabbed her towel. I asked Brian to move so I could clean Layla and separate myself from him. She acted silly as usual just laughing like the towel tickled. Her father laughed right along with her which killed my smile.

The moment felt warm and loving, and I wanted nothing to do with it. Brian would get the wrong idea. He always assumed the best when he saw an ounce of promise, and there wasn't any.

"It's okay for you to laugh, Denise." "I know that," I snapped.

"But you keep...nevermind. I'll get out of your hair, okay?"

"Fine with me."

After staring for a few seconds longer, Brian left the bathroom. In the bedroom, I rubbed Layla down with Aquaphor to keep her eczema under control. When dressed, I led her into the living room where Debbie and Brian were eating dinner.

Debbie offered to make me a plate again. I declined but asked if she could feed Layla because I wanted to lie down. She agreed and took her granddaughter to the kitchen.

Brian watched me the entire time. His gaze was desperate for acknowledgment. I told everyone goodnight and returned to the room. My feelings were mixed about the man I married. Over the past year, he had become a familiar stranger.

CHAPTER FIVE

Brian

"Give her time. She will fight you as long as she can. You know what you did and how it destroyed your wife. All you can do is give her time to make her way back to you," my mom said from my kitchen.

Denise moved into her apartment two weeks ago, and I hadn't been invited there yet. She wouldn't let me help her move in. The only way I spent time with Layla was at Mom's house. Denise would drop her off before I got there, and I'd miss her each time. That woman did a perfect job ducking me.

"How long do I have to wait? A year is long enough. I want my wife, Mom. What I did will forever be the hardest thing to get over, but come on. She knows I will never ever cheat on her again," I fumed while grabbing my plate.

"Does she?" The face Mom gave me forced me to remember she was also a woman who'd gone through the same situation as my wife. How the hell did I miss that?

I fought all my life to be the opposite of my father. The only thing I worried about was not being a deadbeat. Being a cheater never correlated my faults to his. Mom hadn't compared me to him in that aspect, and neither did I —until now.

I was him.

The cheater. The heart breaker. The one that tore down the woman that loved me because I chose not to control my temptation. I'd become that guy. It didn't matter if it was one time with one woman. It was bad enough the woman was Kim, but I did exactly what he did.

My heart still belonged to my wife, and the "other woman" wasn't in the picture outside of taking care of my daughter. I wanted to make things right and to fix my wrongs. I wanted forgiveness and a chance to rebuild.

But what about my wife?

Denise loved and trusted me. I took it for granted. Now, I was barking around her like she owed me forgiveness. What the hell was wrong with me?

"Mom, I don't want to be that guy."

"What guy, baby?"

"Him." I couldn't say his name. I didn't have to. Mom pressed her lips together. She understood.

"Brian, look at me and listen carefully. You are *not* your father, and you never will be. Now, you made similar mistakes, but you are not running from them. You've owned them and are working to clean up your mess. That man had no heart. You have the biggest one. Maybe even too big."

I narrowed my eyes in confusion.

"You just giving it away to one too many women is what I mean. You had feelings for Kim and for a brief, thoughtless moment, you gave in to them. She was as wrong as you, but the two of you owned up to it. I cannot believe she is the mother of my grandchild, but such is life.

"You love who you love, and your wife needs to know that she is the only one with your heart. To her, you chose another woman. She doesn't believe that she was ever important to you because of your actions. Denise has to feel that Kim is not who you want. No matter how much you say it, she has to see it to believe it."

"How am I supposed to prove something like that? It's not like I'm with Kim. She has a man and lives in another state. Denise knows nothing is going on with Kim and me."

"Again, son, how do you know that for sure? You have no idea what is going on in her mind. The best thing you can do is practice patience. I trust that Denise will find her way back to you. Dealing with you and Layla, she'll warm up to it."

"Mom, she runs out of here after leaving Layla. She wants nothing to do with me."

"True, but again, patience. Fight for her attention, and you will eventually gain her affection."

"You make it sound so easy."

"It's not. You know I know. But the difference with what I went through is that you want your family. She will notice that."

"I hope you're right."

"I'd better be, or you'll get a divorce and end up having *two* baby mamas."

She bent over laughing and slapped her knee. The term "baby mama" tickled her every time. To Mom, it sounded like an insult. Me having one was already thrown in my face for her to get a chuckle.

"Nah, I will not let that happen."

"I know you won't. Now, eat your food before it gets cold."

A few bites into the baked tilapia, rice pilaf, and green beans, I remembered Kim's flight was next week and reminded my mom. If I would prove anything to Denise, a run-in with Kim could not go down.

Mom suggested that I pick Ava up from Harold and she'd visit with her granddaughter at my house. The one place

Denise steered clear of. If she needed my mom to watch Layla, then both of my daughters could spend time with each other.

The thought of my babies together pushed me to make it happen rather than avoid it. I'd ask to have Layla that weekend as usual and have Mom drop Layla off with me. None of the mothers would know.

ᛈᛈᛈ

KIM TEXTED me last night that they were at their hotel. When I inquired why not at her parents', she claimed she didn't want the doctor dude to sleep in a separate room. She could've kept that to herself.

Ava would spend tonight and tomorrow afternoon with Kim's parents and then I'd get her in the evening until Sunday. This trip was mainly for a lunch meeting that Kim asked for so her doctor dude could talk with me.

My first reaction was to reject the idea, but then I remembered that this dude spent a lot of time with my daughter. I could use this conversation to check him out myself.

Before our so-called meeting, I went to the gym. It had been a couple months since I worked out and it showed. My stamina left me way too soon. It burned me out after thirty minutes. I had no reason to push further, so I quit.

Lifting weights was my go-to after warm-up stretches, but it didn't happen this morning. After some weak attempts, the elliptical and treadmill were more appealing. Once I resume my routine at the gym before work, I won't fall off again.

I ate at the Waffle House near my mom's house, before going home. My mind wouldn't let go of the way my wife looked at me. It was all I imagined while running.

Denise didn't seem as hardened as she was at first, but she definitely hadn't come to a place of forgiveness. Thanks to Layla, I glimpsed a smile or heard a faint laugh, but as soon as Denise noticed my attention on her, she'd shut down.

All I wanted was for my wife to go back to her normal, happy self. That became a hard task whenever I was near. God, I needed help with this one.

I met Kim and the doctor at Razzoo's for lunch. It was Kim's favorite restaurant. The two of them had a table when I arrived. From the waiting area, I saw him pull her in for a kiss. Then she smiled like a little girl. I had never seen her so giddy. Not even with Trent.

Both of them straightened up when they spotted me coming over. As soon as I sat, a waitress placed their drinks on the table. I ordered a water and an appetizer. I had no desire to stay here long enough for a full meal.

Kim immediately asked whether I'd mind if Evan asked some personal questions. It didn't mean I'd answer anything I didn't want to, so whatever.

"Let's not beat around the bush and waste any of our time," he said gesturing at the both of us. "I have fallen in love with this woman next to me and want to stick around. Because you share a daughter with her, I need to know where you and Kim stand from your mouth."

Kim's lingering smile disappeared.

I stared him down to make it clear that I don't give a shit about his insecurities nor his comfort level when it comes to Kim and me. "Look, Ivan. I—"

"Evan. You know my name is Evan."

"Whatever. I am in the process of getting my wife back. She is to me what Kim is to you. I only want to be with my wife. Yes, Kim and I have a connection now, but that is only because of Ava. You ain't gotta worry about me, bruh."

He stared at me like he was trying to read whether I was bullshitting him.

"That sounds good and all, but are you in love with Kim?"

My eyes shot up at hers. Kim's raced to the ceiling, then to his. "I told you before that you didn't need to ask him that."

"I know, babe. I want to hear it from him." He kissed her cheek.

"That question is invalid. I'm in love with my wife."

"And? It didn't stop you from impregnating Kim. So, the validity is there."

Clinching my jaw, I answered. "No. I am not in love with your girl."

"Woman, not my girl," he corrected me.

I let him make it because of Ava's mother. "You got it."

"Yeah, I got *her*. I don't want to get too deep, and the two of you are still holding on to some fantasy of being with each other."

"Babe, I told you it's not like that. Brian and I are only parents."

Evan's hands rested on the table. "But hooking up twice? Plus, you said he wanted more when his wife bailed on him."

What the hell? Why did she tell him?

"And I also told you we moved past it. He is doing the right thing and pursuing his wife," she defended me.

"Only after you rejected him." Evan waved toward me.

"Okay, do you two need privacy? I am sitting right here. If you have anything else to ask me, just do it. Don't talk like I ain't right in front of you."

"You're right. My fault. Kim told me about you guys' history which is why she wanted us to meet up. The whole college thing and then the cheating part. The attempt to choose her over your wife. Those are red flags. I have love for Kim, but I've been down a similar road with my ex-wife. I'm only trying to avoid a sequel."

"I get it. Kim also told me about *your* last situation."

He turned toward her, and she met his gaze with confidence. "Yes, I told him. Brian is like family. Look, what happened between us was wrong, and we know it. Our goal now is to raise our daughter but have otherwise separate lives."

"Evan, I'm not a threat. Like Kim said, we made a mistake. Now, we have Ava. If it weren't for her, we wouldn't be having this conversation. So, no, I am not in love with your woman. I am in love with my wife. You are free to love her as much as she deserves and more. I love her like family because of our friendship and because of Ava. That's it. You have my word."

Again, he stared hard and long until the tension in his shoulders released.

"Are you good now?" Kim asked him.

"Yeah, I think so. Thanks for meeting up with us. I guess I let everything get to me more than it should have." Evan extended his hand over the table. I shook it.

"It's all good. Kim and I created a mess. I never thought it crept up in y'all relationship too. But I get it. To be honest, I wasn't really a fan of yours." His brow hiked, and Kim laughed. I continued, "You know, being around my daughter so much. I know Kim trusts you and it should be enough, but I didn't like some random dude with my kid."

"Evan is not some random dude, Brian."

"I know that now. I understand that you guys are getting serious. But that little girl is my world and—"

"You don't even have to say it. Ava has already won my heart like her mother has. I will never come between you and her. I will be there for both of them as long as Kim allows. Look at it this way, while you are here and we are home, trust that I will protect them both with my life. I got you on that one."

"Damn." I laughed. "I never thought of that. Perhaps it's not so bad you're around."

"Okay! You both want the same thing. Ava has a big enough heart for all of us to love and protect her. No one has anything to worry about. Are we good? I want to eat in peace."

The waitress came out with our food. They had entrées. She asked if we needed anything else. I requested a drink since the heavy part of this lunch was over. I ordered fried catfish, too. We needed to get better acquainted now that this man promised to be there for my daughter in my absence.

By the end of the meal, I liked the dude. He was good for Kim, and I could tell she loved him. I was happy for her and even envied them. She came out of our ordeal and found happiness. I hoped to do the same.

CHAPTER SIX

FINALLY! THE TENSION BETWEEN TWO OF THE MOST important men in my life disappeared. After the hard part, they got along like no problem ever existed. The guys talked mostly to each other and somewhat ignored me. I gladly sat back and listened.

Anytime Ava came up, both of them lit up with pride. My baby girl was the answer to these men's issue with one another. The conversation even ventured off to basketball. Brian obviously devoted his allegiance to the Rockets, and Evan claimed the Golden State Warriors. He admitted to jumping on the wagon a few years ago, but represented them all the way now.

The waitress brought our check. Evan insisted that he pay. He felt like an asshole for what he thought of Brian before this meeting. Once she returned, I placed the leftovers in a container. She also handed me a bag with the to-go dessert that I had to wait to devour later. I stuffed my face enough for the hour.

While lost in those two going back and forth, I felt someone watching me. It was so strong that it broke my attention away from the men. Once I looked up, I saw Trent pointing at me while guiding his mother's sightline toward our table.

Her face grew into a surprised smile as she made her way over. I froze and didn't have time to warn Brian. My ex-fiancé and basically Brian's ex-friend followed Sheryl's lead from the hostess stand.

"Oh, my goodness, girl! When did you get in town?" she asked from behind Brian.

I stood up, and Brian turned around to see who spoke to me. He returned a worrisome glance my way.

"Brian?" Trent said, taken aback. Sheryl even stopped in her tracks before embracing me.

Trent and Brian gave each other an awkward dap. I assumed Trent's wheels were spinning from his squinted gaze.

"What are you doing here?—Oh! Hi, I'm Sheryl." She greeted the only stranger at the table.

"I'm Evan." He shook her hand.

"Yeah, Evan's my boyfriend," I said, avoiding Trent's eyes. They were fixed on me.

Once I caved and glanced at him, he smirked.

Sheryl gave Evan a once-over. "Well, it's nice to meet you."

"Likewise." He offered that gorgeous smile of his.

Trent nodded to my man, who reciprocated. There were so many elephants in here. We needed to make this reunion as short as possible.

Before I opened my mouth to tell everyone we were heading out, Sheryl opened hers. "Evan, huh?" She squinted at me, then back at him, and finally gasped. "Oh! You must be Ava's father. He's handsome, girl."

"I'm not Ava's dad. He is." When Evan gestured toward Brian, I wanted to somehow disappear or transport my ass far from here.

All the damn time we spent together, I barely mentioned Trenton. Evan only knew that I was once engaged to a man who I'd been with for eight years in a not-so-great relationship. I didn't care to share anything more. I couldn't remember if I'd ever spoken his name in conversations with Evan. Now, I wished I did. He had no clue what he'd done.

"What?" Sheryl yelped.

"What the fuck did he say?" Trenton stood back. Both of them drew attention to our table.

"Shit," Brian mumbled.

Evan stared at me with his head tilted. "Babe, what's going on?"

"Brian, tell me this nigga is jokin'."

"Nigga?" Evan repeated. He hated that word.

"Trent, chill." Brian turned in his seat to stand.

Sheryl placed her hand on my shoulder. "Kim, I-I don't understand."

"It's time for us to go," I told everyone. I grabbed Evan's hand to get up. A large group heading to their table blocked the stairs behind us.

The only way out was past Sheryl and then Trent. I made it around her and ignored her calling my name. Once I got close enough to Trent, he grabbed my arm and damn near yanked me toward him.

"Kim? What the fuck?" Trent yelled.

Evan broke Trent's grasp and pushed him back. "Don't grab her like that, bruh?"

"Nigga, I'll fucking ki—"

"I'm not yo' nigga." Evan stepped forward.

"Whoa! Babe, no!" I tried to get in front of him, but he wouldn't let me. I'd never seen him act this way.

Trent looked like he was about to charge at Evan, but Brian blocked him.

"Nah, man. Let's not do—"

"Man, fuck you." Trent pushed Brian into the table almost knocking it down. Sheryl screamed because the glasses tipped over and spilled her way. She yelled at Trent to stop, but his temper blinded him.

The manager came over along with some customers who tried to help me diffuse things. Evan would not back down. Once I got through, I grabbed his face and made him look at me. The fire in his eyes dwindled, and I recognized him again. "Let's go, now!"

Evan rushed through bystanders as we made it to the doors. The day couldn't have been more beautiful. The sun shined bright, people fed the fish in the lake at the boardwalk behind the restaurant, others gathered around having a good time. But we stood near a tree outside the front entrance, staring at each other.

He looked like he wanted me to say something but I couldn't. No words could explain any of it. Then Trent's voice got louder before he walked through the same doors. Sheryl trailed him, and Brian came out last. The manager stood at the entrance once everyone was outside. I guess he wanted to make sure neither of us would try to re-enter.

Sheryl stood closer to the Kim Son restaurant on the other side of the walkway. Trent walked toward Kim Son's outdoor area until we couldn't see him anymore. Brian stood near us, but no one spoke. He handed me the bag of food I left on the table.

Evan attempted to read me like he always did. I broke from his stare and saw Sheryl looking our way. I mouthed, "I'm sorry."

The confusion still covered her face. Trent headed back toward Sheryl before he noticed us still standing there. Once he did, I wished we weren't.

"You fucked my girl?" He laughed eerily. "No wonder you were always in our business trying to fuck everything up."

"It wasn't even—"

"Spare me, my nigga. You had a baby with my woman."

I held onto Evan in case he felt the need to step in. This had nothing to do with him. I forced him to look at me. "Let's go." He nodded, and we turned to leave.

"Oh! Ohhhh. And you? You acted like I was some dog for messing with a few girls and you were literally fucking my best friend behind my back."

As much as I wanted to correct him, I had to let it go and leave. Trent jogged over to block our path.

"Nah, don't run. Admit that you—"

"Don't say shit to her. Walk away. My patience is wearing thin with your little show. Back up."

Trent ran up on Evan, who had already pushed me out of the way. Trent swung, missed, then tripped. In a blink of an eye, Evan punched him on the jaw. Once Trent balanced himself, he tackled Evan, but they were still on their feet.

A crowd gathered around us, anticipating a show I assumed. Not on my watch. The manager at Razzoo's mentioned that he'd call the police. Brian held me back because I wanted to stop them. "You will only get hurt, Kim. Let them stop on their own."

"Brian, I don't want them fighting."

"These are grown ass men. What are you gonna do?"

"Trenton, stop it!" Sheryl demanded to her rage- fueled son. He focused on Evan, and vice versa. The Kim Son wall stopped their tussling. Evan's back was against the restaurant's exterior, and he pushed Trent off.

When Evan stepped away from the building, he squared up ready for whatever else Trent would throw.

I broke from Brian's grasp and ran between them. Once close enough to Evan, I pulled him along on the way to the car. I told him to get inside. He hesitated. I had to scream at him to get his attention. When we made eye contact, he did what I asked.

At the hotel, Evan said nothing. He hadn't spoken a word

since we drove off from Razzoo's parking lot. I left him in the room to go to my parents' house. We were supposed to go together so Evan could meet my mom.

Last night, we had dinner with my siblings' families and my dad. Keisha thought it would be better if Evan met the sane members of my family before introducing him to our mother. It turned out to be a great night.

Kendrick and my brother-in-law, Andrew, sat on the porch with Evan and my father after we finished dinner. Daddy already met him in California, so at least Evan knew one person out there.

The girls and I got all caught up and cut the pecan pie my sister-in-law made. We topped each slice with ice cream. Once we realized the men were having too much fun, we put their pieces in the freezer so the ice cream wouldn't melt. We finished half of our dessert by the time they came in all loud.

After dessert, Daddy went home since he'd left Mom on her own with Ava and my nephews long enough. He reminded me how much he liked Evan when I walked him outside. He acted exactly like Aunt Viv about Evan.

When we headed out, the guys exchanged numbers and made plans to connect some kind of way. I loved seeing my baby laugh and enjoy himself with my crazy people. Not one second did he seem uncomfortable or out of place.

Today, however, was a different story. Keisha chilled at my parents' house with Daddy and Ava before Brian came over. I needed to show him how to properly install Ava's car seat.

Brian apologized for the earlier incident. We were both in shock. He told me he left soon after we did and before the cops arrived, if ever called.

Evan looked like he would have killed Trent. It disappointed me that he didn't walk away from the fight. Brian tried to take Evan's side and told me I should be happy I got a man willing to fight for me. Evan never came out of pocket before. The anger in his eyes scared me.

Back inside, we explained to everyone what happened at the restaurant. Luckily, Mom had gone to her room. If she heard any of this, I'd never live it down. Drama clung onto me like I was a damn reality TV star. I couldn't catch a break. Every single time I stepped a foot in this city, I paid for it in some way.

When I returned to our hotel room, all the lights were out. There was no way he'd fallen asleep this damn early.

"Evan?" I said after removing my shoes and sitting on the bed.

"Yeah," he responded dryly.

"You want to talk about today?"

"Do you?"

"I mean, not really. Then again, we need to clear things up while we still can. I don't want you running with assumptions about anything."

He flipped over to face me. "Then talk."

That tone of his might get him cussed out. I had to remember that today was on me though. "Okay...Where do I even start?"

"How about your ex! Talk about why shit went left so fast."

I swallowed hard and shook my hands at my waist to make sure I didn't say anything we'd both regret. "You're upset. I understand that, but don't cuss at me. How was I supposed to—"

"Kim, I'm sorry. It's hard sometimes with you. I can't always tell if you are honest about your past and your relationships with all these men."

"What men, Evan? I hadn't been with any other guy while with Trent. There are no men."

"You mean besides Brian. Your ex's best friend, Kim? I believe you left that part out."

"No, I didn't. We were all best friends. I told you that. I've been honest with you."

Evan sat up revealing his bare upper body. "How many times have you slept with Brian?"

I groaned. "Are we really doing this again? I told you everything before, Evan. Why is it different now?"

"It's different when dudes run up on me yelling that their friend fucked their woman with a motive. Maybe it's been going on longer than you want to admit."

"You know what? I will give you more time to calm down. I don't even recognize you right now."

"Yeah, likewise." He laid back down facing away.

A good old-fashioned "fuck you" sat on the tip of my tongue, but I had to bite it. I did not want to talk to him that way. I made that mistake with Trent and then his disrespectful side showed out every time we fought. He must've thought it was fair game because of my mouth.

With Evan, I never had to go there. I guess you can't really know someone in the short time we'd been together. He probably had a lot of shit about him that I wouldn't like. Trust issues were obvious based on his cheating wife. We overcame that one. At least I thought so.

Brian was a soft subject. Although they got along earlier today, Evan's attitude proved that it wouldn't be enough for him to get past what we'd done.

I spent the night at Keisha and Andrew's house. My dumb ass got so mad that I took nothing with me. Luckily, my sister and I wore the same size. They also had toiletries to spare. Once my nephew was down, we watched *Blackish* until falling asleep on the couch.

CHAPTER SEVEN

On the way to her house, Mom texted that Denise dropped Layla off. Perfect timing. I wanted to miss a run-in with Denise while I had Ava.

I pulled up in the driveway and Mom opened the door holding Layla. Her gracious smile showed how much she missed Ava. God blessed me with the most forgiving and understanding mother.

Kim used to talk about how much she wished Mrs. Duncan took a lesson or two from my mom or even Sheryl when it came to accepting their children. She expressed how her mother was only super hard on her and not her siblings. It made me appreciate this beautiful woman more.

The fact that I ended up with two kids close in age by my wife and Kim could have strained our relationship for a minute. After simply expressing disappointment, she never missed a beat. Mom stepped right into proud grandmother mode.

We swapped babies. Mom hugged Ava and gave her a dozen kisses on her cheeks. Ava giggled. I tossed her little back-pack in the hall on the way to the living room. Then we all got on the floor. Well, Mom put Ava on the floor and eased herself onto the couch.

"Wow! Those are your babies."

"Yeah, they are. Crazy, huh?"

I put them close together before snapping a few pictures with my phone. This was only the second time they'd been in the same room since I found out I had a second daughter. A tear tried to fall, but once my mom's eyes welled up, I pulled myself together.

"Man, what a beautiful sight."

"Boy, isn't it? I got *two* grandbabies!" The smile on her face was everything. She understood how difficult things had been because of these two angels, but I wouldn't have it any other way. I loved them too much to regret any of it.

Mom had plenty of toys on the floor for them, and I turned on *Bubble Guppies* for the sound since neither of them cared about watching anything. It caught their attention for a few minutes, then they were back at banging blocks together.

"How was your day, son?"

"Eventful. But I don't want to talk about it."

"Well, I wish you would've warned me earlier."

"About what?"

"Child, Sheryl called me all riled up."

"Ah, dang. I didn't even think about that." I took a deep breath. "What did she tell you?"

"She said Kim's man told her the one thing you made me swear to keep to myself."

"Okay, in his defense, he didn't know who he was talking to. He never met them before."

"Why didn't y'all stop him?"

"It happened so fast and so casual. Sheryl assumed Evan was Ava's dad, and he corrected her. That's when shit...Sorry, I mean that's when everything went downhill. Trent popped off, and Evan was trying to stand up for Kim."

"Poor Trent."

"Poor Trent? Nah, Mom, he did too much. This wasn't his business."

"How so? You two grew up together, Brian. Kim was with him for all those years."

I didn't want to hear it. "Trent never respected Kim, so all those years meant nothing."

"Oh, so you are justifying your actions because he was a bad boyfriend? He was like a brother to you."

I sucked my teeth. This day had to come, eventually. She never let me have it before. I guess the grace period had run out.

"You can have an attitude all you want. That boy was your family, and you let some woman come between y'all. It was always wrong even before he found out you made a baby with her. So, if I want to empathize with Trent for having every right to be mad, I will."

"Okay, Mom."

She hopped off the couch and walked to the kitchen searching for something. When she didn't find it, her anger intensified. She wanted to go off on me. Whether I agreed with her or not, I'd take whatever she dished so she could finally get it out.

I distracted myself with the girls while she stared at me from the other side of the room. "I need to go to the store. The girls need snacks. And Denise didn't leave any diapers for Layla."

"You don't have to. I'll go."

"No! Let me. I need to get out of the house before I curse you out."

"Why you so mad at me right now?"

"Because I had to explain to my best friend, why *my* son got *her* son's ex-girlfriend pregnant! She's pissed at me like I did something wrong all because I had to keep *your* secret."

My chest hardened at the thought of my mother defending me to Sheryl. That must've been tough to keep it from her all this time. Shit! Why can't my mess be only mine? Everyone had some kind of backlash over it. I hoped the worst was over once the truth initially came out last year.

"Mom, wait." I got up from the floor and rushed to her. I hugged her tight and lifted her off the floor a few inches. She giggled and fought me off like she always did. Once I put her down, she rested her hands on her hips, still clearly upset.

"I am so, so sorry for everything. I didn't think about any of this the way I should have. And you're right, Trent deserved better from me. It pissed me off that he was trying to fight Kim's dude and now they are in a bad place. We keep messing things up further for everyone around us."

"Well, you are right about him fighting. That was wrong, and he is too damn old for that, but he took a huge blow today. And so did Sheryl. She loved that girl."

"Yeah, I understand. Again, I am really sorry."

"I know you are, baby." She pushed my forehead.

"So, what do you need from the store? I'll pick it up."

"I'll make you a list." Mom walked into the kitchen to get her notepad from a drawer. Someone rang the doorbell.

Layla and Ava were still peacefully playing with the toys on the floor, so I answered the door.

"Oh, hey. I left Layla's bag at home. I tried calling Debbie to tell her I was coming back to drop it off."

I only had the door opened wide enough for me to stand in the threshold so I could block her view of the girls. "Thanks, Denise. I was about to go to the store to get diapers. We just realized she had none."

"Oh, okay."

"So, we'll see you later then. What time are you picking her up?"

"Maybe close to nine. I told your mom she could bathe

51

her and put her in pajamas while she's here. Or you can, but be careful to watch her in the tub."

"Will do." I stood in the doorway and tried to block her sight when she moved her head to peek around me.

"Brian, what are you doing?"

"Nothing. You need something else?"

"Why are you acting weird?"

"Am I? My bad. I guess I am a little tired, but I wanted to spend time with Ava while Mom had her."

Denise's eyes widened. "Ava?"

"No! No, I'm sorry. Layla, I meant Layla. I told you I'm tired. But we will see you at nine, okay?"

Her eyes narrowed when she heard the girls getting louder. Then she pushed me to the side and saw both girls on the floor. "What the hell? Oh naw, we didn't agree to this."

"Denise, please don't overreact. It's okay. They can play together."

She walked over and picked up Layla. "You had Kim around my child?"

"Layla is my daughter too. And no, she was not here. I picked Ava up from her grandparents."

Mom stayed out of it and came to the living room to get Ava.

"Look, it's admirable that the two of you are so cool about doing the right thing. I can't. That little girl, as beautiful and innocent as she is, represents something I am not ready to accept. Debbie, I don't appreciate you lying to get my daughter over here."

"I didn't lie. Denise, please understand that we are not trying to be malicious. Brian only wanted to see them together since he already had Ava for the night."

"I don't see what the problem is. They are sisters whether you want to admit it or not," I snapped.

At that moment, I wished I'd kept my damn mouth shut. That woman was a serial killer with the glares she shot out.

"If I want to admit it? I don't have to admit anything except that fact that moving here was a mistake. You don't want us, you want *them*."

"What? Who is them? Yes, I want my daughters. I am their father. But the only woman I want is you. I promise you that."

"You sure don't act like it with all this sneaking around."

"It's not like you would ever hear me out if I told you beforehand. You want me to hate my daughter because you hate how she got here. I don't like it either, but what's done is done. Trust me. I am not trying to hurt you."

Denise stood in the living room holding Layla as if she was protecting her from surrounding enemies. She tossed her eyes back and forth between my mom and me. I saw her glance at Ava a couple times as my mother tickled her to stop her from getting antsy.

"That little girl right there should not be an obstacle between us. I love her, and I love you and Layla. Does that make me a bad person?"

She didn't answer. Her grip on Layla got tighter after my baby girl reached for me when I approached them. Denise wouldn't let her go.

"I don't like this, Brian. I don't."

"Dee, I understand where you're coming from. But fighting over this is unnecessary. We have to accept that I have another child. She isn't going anywhere. I only get to be with her for short periods between longer ones. I wanted to have this moment to spend with both girls."

For the first time in forever, Dee stared into my eyes with compassion. It seemed like she calmed down and brooded over my point. Then seconds later, she loosened her grip on Layla and let me have her.

My mom handed me Ava. Was she trying to piss Denise off

all over again? The anger rebuilt in my wife's eyes. Before she could react, my mom stood next to her and grabbed onto Denise's shoulders. "Look at this picture. What do you see, Denise? Be honest and tell us why this hurts you."

"Debbie, you know why."

"Yes. But say it anyway."

Denise tried to pull away from my mom, but she held on tighter. The tears fell.

"Mom, stop. That's enough."

"No, Brian. She has to heal, and if she will ever do so, she has to face it all the way." Mom faced my wife. "Tell us, Denise. Whatever comes out is okay. Let it out."

"She's Kim's kid! Okay? I hate Kim for what she did, and I hate you for your part. All I see is pain and a reminder that I wasn't good enough. That you never wanted me. You wanted her."

"Dee, that's not true. You know it's not true."

"No, I don't," she screamed. Both girls jumped a little in my arms. "How could you say that? You slept with the only real friend I had. The one person that introduced us. They were a part of us. We were all like family, and you slept with her.

"How am I supposed to look at this little girl without seeing my husband cheating on me? On me, Brian! I gave you everything, and you threw it away for Kim? Why did you even fucking marry me if you wanted her so bad?

"I don't trust that you didn't always want her instead of me. I don't trust that you had only been with her one time. I don't feel safe with you. Not with my heart or anything else."

The tears covered her cheeks and gathered beneath her chin before falling onto her shirt. She tried to wipe them away, but they were falling faster than her already damped hands could clean up. I had no words to make them stop. Nothing could fix my mistake. It was tangible. I could hold it—*her*—in my arms.

I took a step closer because I wanted to hold Denise. Somehow, I needed to help her. Mom shook her head for me to let Denise be.

"Brian, you told me that Denise should already know that you wouldn't hurt her again. What do you think now?"

When did my mom become a damn therapist? She'd been watching too much *Iyanla, Fix My Life*.

I was a fool for what I said. Not one time did I ever process what Denise really felt about Ava. My innocent baby girl represented so many insecurities that I created for my wife. We hadn't talked about it because Denise usually avoided me, but now we had no choice other than face it. As hard as it was, this may be the only way to move forward.

"I think I ruined the perfect woman for no reason at all. I don't deserve her love or her trust as much as I thought I did. I don't deserve any ounce of kindness because of how I broke our comfort, our marriage, our world apart. Dee, nothing you did made me..."

The word didn't want to come out because it felt ugly. All of this felt more than ugly. I had disgraced my mother's teachings of what kind of man I should be. I disgraced my wife who trusted me to be the man I presented to her daily. My love for her had no bounds, yet I gave myself to another woman so willingly that my body ached at the thought. I cheated. *Cheated*.

"Nothing you did made me...cheat. I acted on old emotions that resurfaced at the wrong time. Feelings I should have never had. They were there before I ever met you and I thought we destroyed them when we fell in love. I always had love for Kim, but I didn't plan to ever act on it. I didn't. I love you. But..."

How could I say this? The whole truth needed to come

out, but my wife was already in pieces. I didn't want to keep piling on top of this mountain between us.

I must've taken too long to finish. "But what?" Denise asked.

"If I'm gonna be completely honest about everything, then...um..."

The thought of the words exiting my lips made me sick. Only because I knew what it would do to my wife. I didn't want to hurt her anymore, but this was the last secret I would keep. Honesty was my only way out.

"Brian, what are you saying?" Denise demanded.

CHAPTER EIGHT

Denise

"Before you and I were ever intimate, I slept with Kim," Brian let out.

"Oh, God." My stomach dropped to the floor. "I knew it! I knew there was something between you two. I should've never—We need to go. It-It's getting late."

Blow after blow from his "honesty" hurt far worse than I wanted to feel. I wish I could be numb to it, but the pain shot through my heart, looped around, and created another hole.

When I pulled away from Debbie, she took my hand into hers. "No, Denise. Y'all have to talk this through. Explain yourself, son."

Brian lowered his head for a few seconds, then gazed at me. "Dee...Look, I liked her more than just as a friend in college. After we did what we did the first time, I chose not to go any further. I chose you. This was before me and you got serious. That's the whole truth." He took a deep breath. "Now you know everything."

Brian finally put the girls down on the couch. They fell asleep in his arms.

I squeezed Debbie's hand and glared at her. "Aren't you a

proud momma? He's so 'matter a fact' as if he has no heart at all. Who says stuff like that?"

"Denise, he's trying. He realizes the errors of his ways. Besides, he wasn't always this calm. A lot of time has passed. That is the only reason he's calm about it. Trust me," Debbie said under her breath.

"Trust you? He's *your* son. You will always take his side."

Brian planted himself in front of me, closer than before. "No, she won't. She was about to go off on me about this before you came. Believe me, she's not happy with me. Neither am I."

I laughed in his face. "Is that supposed to make me feel better?"

"No. I don't know. You said you didn't trust me, so I am trying to be transparent."

"Good for you, Brian. I hope that helps you sleep at night but it damn sure doesn't help me. If you two don't mind, I want to go home and rest. I've had about enough for today. Layla's already out, so..." I shrugged my shoulders with nothing more to say.

"How about you go lie down in the back room? We will take care of Layla so you can rest. I don't want you driving. You look like you want to strangle someone. I don't want you too distracted to focus on the road," Brian requested.

He must have also known he'd be the one I'd strangle. The nerve of him to tell me he slept with her twice and act like it was water under the bridge. Not my bridge. There was no water beneath. It was dry with big ass sharp rocks, and I wanted to push him off.

Brian chose not to go any further? Then how the fuck did they end up having a kid together? He lied to himself in the past, and he was lying now.

"I cannot stay here with you."

"If you want to leave that bad, I will take you home."

"So, yeah, the whole not wanting to stay here with you probably didn't register. I don't want to be in a car with you either, Brian. I need space."

Brian's eyes rolled dramatically. "Space? You've been gone over a year, Denise. Damn!" He put his hands over his face and took a few deep breaths, then slightly raised his hands up. "I want you, but if you need me to back off, I will."

He gave Layla a kiss and picked up Ava. "Mom, I will see you tomorrow before I have to take Ava back. Denise, I'm sorry. It will never be enough, but I'm still sorry. Get home safe."

Brian scooped up a pink backpack and walked out the door. Debbie excused herself and escorted him to his car.

I made my attempt to run for it before Debbie came back inside, but she caught me walking toward the door. "You sure you don't want to stay? I don't mind."

"I'm positive. We will be fine. I'll text you when we get in, okay?"

Debbie lowered her eyes before suddenly perking up with a plastered smile. "Okay, baby. Be careful."

I nodded and finally got the hell out of there. The temptation to call Momma on the way home was heavy. In the back of my mind, I believed she'd agree with them. My parents pleaded for months for me to try again with Brian or at least let him near Layla. One out of two was as good as it would get.

When we got home, I skipped Layla's bath and let her sleep. I took a shower and jumped under the covers. My bedroom didn't have a TV, and I needed a distraction. The bed was too comfortable to get up, so I watched Hulu on my phone.

Debbie put me on to *Designated Survivor*. We watched it when I stayed with her. It took me back to when we used to faithfully watch *24* together. I put the show on where we left off. In the middle of an episode, a text notification rudely interrupted the show.

Lying Asshole: Do you want a divorce?

Me: Can we not do this now?

Lying Asshole: We have to. I can't stop thinking about you, but clearly, you still hate me. Tell me what you want to do.

Me: I want to be left alone.

When Brian didn't respond, I let out a sigh of relief. He finally listened. Now, I could return to the show. Two minutes later, another interruption.

Lying Asshole: If you really knew how much I love you, we could be happy again.

Me: Too much has happened for me to ever be truly happy with you.

Lying Asshole: So, that's it? I don't get another chance?

Since he was pissing me off, I'd do the same. It took a minute to figure out what to say. After this, I would probably turn off my phone and go to sleep.

Me: Look at the bright side. Now you can move to wherever your girl is. You can have what you always wanted. Her.

That must have struck a nerve. Brian said nothing. I hit play on my phone to finish the last twenty minutes of an episode. I prayed he wouldn't text back. Before I reached Amen, my phone buzzed again.

Lying Asshole: I really hope you can forgive me one day. Even if you divorce me. And fyi, Kim has someone in her life. I didn't like him and he had a problem with me until we sat down and talked everything out. People still do that these days. Talk. That's how they get through issues. I only wished you could give me the same chance that Kim's man did.

Lying Asshole: And for the record, she is not my girl. You are. You were. I hope we can co-parent like adults since that's apparently all we'll ever be.

Lying Asshole: I will leave you alone now

Brian and his long ass texts. I didn't appreciate him trying to act like Kim having a man wasn't the reason he wasn't with her. That guy probably blocked Brian from who he really wanted.

Who cared if he fixed issues with some guy? He wasn't married to him or cheat and try to minimize it all. Whatever their problem was, had no comparison to our own.

Luckily, he left me alone. I watched two full episodes before calling it a night. I checked on Layla and changed her. She was too sleepy to notice anything which meant I'd have an early morning once she'd finally wake up.

Back in bed with everything off, I wondered if Brian couldn't sleep. Whenever anything bothered him, even the smallest thing, he'd lose sleep over it.

Going over the evening in my mind, I understood that Brian was sincere and forthcoming with the belief I'd change how I felt. It hurt me the tiniest bit to see him leave the way he did.

I hadn't witnessed him go through any of the emotions I drowned myself in when I left. He still struggled in his own way. Good.

CHAPTER NINE

Evan would leave to go back home late in the evening. Since we spent last night apart, today was the only time he'd be able to meet my mother. I wasn't in a rush for their introduction.

We had enough drama for the weekend so far. Knowing how that woman could get, it would only go further south. Daddy promised she'd be on her best behavior, but his track record with keeping her in check was sketchy.

I left Keisha's house when they got ready for church. I opted out on her invitation to join them. Instead, I went to get breakfast from the Waffle House on West Airport. I had half a mind to eat there and do whatever else I wanted to avoid Evan. There were too many people inside to get a table for one.

I ordered my pecan waffle with eggs and bacon. I got Evan the same, but with sausage and a plain waffle. Once I paid, I did the grown-up thing and headed to the hotel.

When I got into the room, Evan was sitting on the bed fully dressed minus shoes. He turned the TV off and put the remote on the nightstand. I saw the remorse in his eyes. He texted me a few times last night, but I didn't read any of them. Fighting over text wasn't my thing.

Evan cleared his throat. Before he could say anything, I gave him his food and condiments. I ate mine at the desk with headphones on and watched *The Breakfast Club* on YouTube.

Evan thanked me for bringing him breakfast, but I pretended not to hear him. He called my name twice after I finished half of my waffle. That was about as far as I usually got if I finished the eggs and bacon first, which I did.

His hand touched my shoulder. I couldn't ignore him anymore. Pulling off the headphones, I stood up to throw away my trash.

"You need something?" I asked when he didn't say anything.

He dropped his head. "I feel like such an asshole."

I looked up at him after falling onto the bed. "You should."

Our eyes locked. "Babe, you gotta be straight with me."

"When have I not been?"

He nodded before scratching his chin. "Explain what yesterday was about."

Like he hadn't figured it out. With all the time on his hands last night, he knew. "The woman that approached us was my ex's mother, and we were close. I talked to her a lot even after the breakup. I considered her a friend."

"Not so much to tell her the truth though?"

I narrowed my eyes. "Evan, you understand the situation with Brian and me. It's not something I go around bragging about. Sheryl knows about Ava, but no, I didn't tell her who her father was. It literally wasn't her business. She once believed Trent was the father, but I cleared that up, and we hadn't talked about it since.

"Yes, my ex and Brian were close friends. I did not cheat on him though. We were already over. Trent had moved on with other women by the time Brian and I…Yesterday, you let the cat out of the bag to the two people we agreed to keep in the dark. We thought it was too much to have them know what we did and wanted to spare them."

"Sounds like you wanted to protect yourselves."

"Maybe. Either way, now it's out."

"Yeah, it is. The other thing I don't understand is why you would tell Brian anything about my past relationship? Kim, there has to be a line. Don't talk to him about me or us. Ava should be your only topic."

"Why? We are still friends, Evan."

He released his breath abruptly. "Friends who cheated. You on your best friend and him on his wife. I don't like you talking to him about anything personal. I just don't."

Evan's head dropped again. "I'm not trying to be hard on you, but damn. It's always something with your past. It hits too close to home. I don't always know how to handle it. You know what I went through with my ex-wife and sometimes you do the same stuff she did."

"Evan, I would never do what she did to you. I only want you, and if I don't tell you something, it's because I don't think it's important. I don't do it to keep secrets. That never worked out well for me anyway. With you, I want things to be different."

"You have to do better, Kim. Let me in on things. I realize you are not my ex, but like I said, some of those same feelings creep up when I feel you aren't honest."

"Okay. It won't happen again. We won't talk about anything else personal. I'm sorry. But you should've kept your cool yesterday."

His head jerked back. "What did I do?"

"I don't need you fighting anyone over this mess, Evan. You could've gone to jail."

He pulled me up from the bed and wrapped his arms

around me. "I don't give a damn where I would've ended up. No one will grab you or disrespect you in my presence. I don't get down like that. As your man, it's my job to protect you."

My heart sped up, and a warmth flowed through me. "You sure you still want to be my man? You were pretty pissed at me." I pouted.

He chuckled. "Don't make that face, Kim. I love you. Yes, you can piss me off sometimes, but that doesn't make me love you any less. As long as you are straight with me, we'll be good."

I leaned my head against his chest. "I'm sorry about the drama. I told you I hated coming here and now you see why. Some dumb shit always pops off. I mean you were fighting."

"Ah, that was nothing. Just a little scuffle. You don't want to see me really fight. It might scare you."

My eyes widened, and so did his smile. "The doctor fights? Who are you?"

"Your man. Don't let that white jacket fool you. I will drop a nigga if I have to."

I gasped. "I thought you hated that word."

"I was raised to hate it as we all should. But sometimes—"

"Sometimes a nigga gotta get dropped." I finished for him. We laughed so hard that he let go of me.

"Damn, I love you. With all that you come with, I still can't let go of you." Evan pulled me into him again and planted the softest kiss on my lips.

I gently bit his bottom lip then leaned back. "We'll see about that after you meet the judge today."

He laughed. "Your mother can't be that bad."

"Yeah, okay. I hope you're right. Maybe you will put a better taste in her mouth when it comes to me. To her, I failed at life already."

"Don't worry about that. But about putting a taste in someone's mouth. Let's explore that a little more."

"You nasty!" I giggled before he kissed me.

Evan slid his hands up my shirt and underneath my bra. "Babe, we gotta get Ava soon."

"Okay," he whispered into my neck, planting a kiss there. My bra unclasped on the first attempt. Evan lowered his hands onto my ass. He paused and then rubbed around the outside of my sister's jogging pants she let me have after my shower this morning. He cocked up his brow. "You're not wearing..."

"I didn't have any clean ones with me after my shower. That was one thing I would not borrow."

The way he looked at me made me wish I had panties on. The wetness that leaked had nowhere to go. A little got onto the crotch of the pants. "Now, Ava most definitely has to wait. Her mama up in here tryna get it." He grabbed a handful of my bare ass and pushed my pants down. I stepped out of them.

"You're the one who can't—" Evan picked me up and forced my legs around his waist.

"Let me show you that I'm still your man."

The moisture between my legs doubled. Evan had this innocent, good guy aura about him, but when he wanted me, he'd say shit that made me think it was a front.

We fell onto the bed, and his lips met mine again. Closing my eyes, I offered my tongue. He accepted it with a swipe of his own. My breathing became heavy. His kisses did more to me than any man's ever had. If he only knew how he made my body feel, no man from my past would ever put doubt in his heart.

With one swoop, he'd removed my shirt and already unfastened bra. "I love you, Kim."

I looked into his eyes. "I love you more."

"You wanna bet." That smirk on his face meant trouble.

"As a matter of fact, I do." I rolled over on top of him and damn near ripped off his clothes.

Starting at his neck, my lips brushed against his skin trailing to his chest. His dick tapped me with every touch. When I swiped my lips near his belly button, he yanked me back up so that we were face to face.

"Nah, me first," he said, serving me his tongue.

I broke away from his lips. "That's what I'm trying to do."

He flashed that sexy ass smile. "Quit playing. I gotta taste you first."

I shook my head. "Not today." I lowered myself, but he stopped me.

"Evan...let me—" Our tongues danced with the addition of his soft moans. I took his arms from my waist and slammed them on the pillow where his head rested. "Babe, I made a mess of things, and I want to make it up to you. Let me have this one."

"That's the plan, but your stubborn ass won't listen." Just like that, I was back on the bottom. Evan hovered over me, kissing me hard. He nibbled on my ear. "We good. I got you."

I let him think so and finally relaxed. He backed away to take me all in. His gaze brought every ounce of my juices to the edge. Evan adored me in a way I thought no one could. "Damn, you're so sexy," he whispered.

Evan caressed my breasts with one hand. Those hands. So big and strong, but they touched my body with such care.

My nipples could cut glass. He noticed it too. They pointed right at him more intently when he touched them.

I closed my eyes once his mouth covered my left areola. His tongue circled my nipples in between sucks. My moans were getting louder as I gyrated my hips at the warmth of his mouth on my body. I wanted him inside me.

"Babe..." I begged.

"Patience, Kim." He loved teasing me. I hated it because he saw me unravel too many times before we did the real thing.

That tongue of his was dangerous. Just the sensation of

the smallest connection on my body sent ripples all over, and they usually ended right where I wanted him to be.

Evan squeezed my breasts as he flickered his tongue between the soft licks and sucks. My body squirmed beneath his as my first orgasm released. He tugged at my nipples with his teeth as I rode the wave.

Once it stopped, he kissed his way lower. My attempt to make him come first had failed, but I still wanted to have the first taste.

I reached between us and grabbed his dangling, erect goodness. He quivered at my touch. "Mmm, what are you doing?"

I answered with slow strokes before reaching further to caress his scrotum. "Mmm." Got him.

Without letting go, I pushed him onto his side and then to his back and straddled him. "Kim..." his voice dragged. His eyes were closed as my hands squeezed around his shaft in an up and down motion. "Damn, baby," he whispered.

I kissed the tip, and he let out another moan. He wasn't the only one who could tease. Before I did my thing, I wanted him to wait. Licking my lips for added moisture, I kissed a trail from the tip to the base with my mouth partly open, so he'd feel a little tongue with each kiss. "Shit!"

At the base, my tongue came out to play. I slowly licked my way back to the head and put my mouth around it for a quick suck. His hips elevated briefly. I repeated the licking trail two more times before taking him into my mouth.

Evan raised his hand to his forehead as I deep throated him in the worst way. All the sounds he made and the way he felt in my mouth made me release again. I never came while giving head, but with Evan, I was turned on to the max every damn time.

I must've gone too wild with it while losing it myself because he damn near yelled. My mouth strokes sped up, and the sucks strengthened as I fought through releasing the third time.

"Fuck. Fuck!" he said before I felt his warm cream shoot to the back of my throat. I had no choice but to swallow it. It came out so fast. That was a first. "Fuck, Kim. What are you trying to do to me?"

I didn't even want him to reciprocate, I wanted him inside me. I got up to get a condom from his suitcase. After handing it to him, he appeared bemused. "I need a minute. Then it's your turn."

Thinking he'd be ready soon after, I laid next to him. Minutes later, we were both knocked out.

CHAPTER TEN

KIM CALLED AND ASKED ME TO MEET HER AT HER parents' later than planned. Mom came over this morning instead of church because she wanted to say goodbye to Ava. Since my daughter had a few extra hours with us, we took her to the park.

"Why would you put that option in her head? She will now most likely take it," Mom badgered me about the texts I sent Denise last night.

"It ain't like that's not where all this is going, Mom. She will never forgive me. I wouldn't be so stupid ever again in life, but I can't hold on to her if she is pulling away."

"You were all 'I will fight for my wife. I will do whatever it takes' a week ago. How can you just give up now?"

"Do you see another way? I don't. When she was with her parents, I had all these plans on how I'd win her back if I could ever get close to her again. Now that she's near, I see firsthand how much she despises me. Even if there is a glimmer of hope, she swallows it and turns cold. I told you she said she could never be happy with me. What am I supposed to do with that?"

Mom put Ava in a toddler swing and pushed. "Son, the only thing I can say is fight until you lose. You haven't lost her yet."

What was she talking about? I didn't know what lenses Mom looked through, but things were pretty clear from what I saw from my wife. Denise completely forced me out of her life and was determined to keep it that way.

"If she hated you so much, she would not be here. Believe me. Hate would keep the distance, but she came back. Even if she doesn't act like it, there is still a chance for you two. It may be small right now. However, I believe if you keep pushing, she will slowly let her guard down."

"Mom, even if any of that is true, how am I supposed to break through if she avoids me every chance she gets? I can't get enough time with her to push as you say."

"Boy, if you don't stop acting like you got a restraining order or something. Pop up at her house, send her gifts, offer to help her with things until she finally accepts. When I say push, I mean—"

"Stalk." I laughed so hard once she slapped me upside my head.

"I was gonna say show up even when she doesn't ask you to."

"So, you *want* to make her put a restraining order out on me."

"She will not do that to you. If she does..." Mom slowed the swing and covered Ava's ears. "I'll kick that heifer's ass myself."

We laughed at her punching and kicking the air to show me what she'd do.

The three of us spent another thirty minutes at the park, then we took Ava to Gringo's off US-59. Mom loved that place, and it was early enough to beat the church crowd.

After lunch, I drove a tipsy grandma home. Mom threw

back three margaritas like lemonade. I warned her, but she's grown as she always felt the need to remind me. Well, now her grown butt had tipped off to sleep during the ten-minute drive home.

I made her a pot of coffee so she could stay awake until we left. Ava kept her up for sure with all the loud screams and giggles. We played a version of hide-and-seek. I stayed in the same spot behind the couch while Ava peeked her head to see me and squealed. It never got old to her, and it tickled my mom too.

After an hour, Mom said her final goodbye to Ava until the next time she came here or whenever we go to Cali. She smothered Ava with so many kisses that my baby girl took off running once she got down. Mom chased her a little, but Ava shot around the house with a quickness. My poor mother didn't stand a chance.

I arrived at Kim's parents' house and parked near the curb. I texted Kim that we made it, but she wasn't there yet. A minute later, she pulled into the driveway. Harold opened the front door and came out to greet all of us.

"Daddy, what are you doing home? Wasn't there another church service?" Kim asked surprised.

Harold dipped his chin, giving up the people's eyebrow. "I have a one service maximum. Me and Jesus are good. He don't need to see me that many times in one day."

We laughed. I dapped Evan and Ava reached for him. It still annoyed me slightly, but my baby knew I was her dad. Besides, he was a good dude.

"Shame. Well, how long do we have before she gets home?" Kim inquired for all our sakes.

"A while. The service started maybe thirty minutes ago. Y'all come on inside. I barbecued a lil somethin', somethin'." Harold winked at us.

Kim's nose wrinkled as the aroma hit us. "Ooh, Daddy. That's you?"

I assumed this was a family affair. "I'll see you guys next time."

Harold stopped walking toward the door. "You're not coming?"

"No, sir. I already ate."

"Alright. More smoked boudain for Kim."

"Smoked boudain! Thanks, Daddy. I'll take all of it."

I lifted my hands as if in surrender. "I can come in real quick for a to-go plate. Wouldn't want it to go to waste if you made too much, you know."

Harold's grin grew into a chuckle. "That's what I thought. Y'all come in before the neighbors catch us and ask for food."

Kim pointed at him. "You like it when they do. They always brag on Harold's pit skills."

Harold told us to have a seat in the living room while he checked on the food. Kim joined him after telling her man that she'd get him a link of boudain. Evan's face gave away his confusion. "You never had it, huh?" I asked him.

"Never heard of it." We laughed.

"That's one of Kim's favorite foods." Evan's eyes narrowed my way. "Hey, I only know because of years of friendship. She and my wife are obsessed with any form of boudain. Especially, boudain balls. You can loosen up, man."

"My bad. This weekend got my mind everywhere."

"Yeah, yesterday was insane. You handled yours though."

He cracked a smile. From his stance with Trent, he knew what he was doing. "Had to be weird for you. I wasn't trying to come at yo' boy. Kim's safety was my number one concern. Dude seemed a little off grabbing her. I don't like that kind of shit."

"I hear you. We're probably done for real this time. My

mom was on my back about it too. Kim and I screwed things up for ourselves, and everyone involved. Even indirectly."

"My bad for telling them about Ava. I didn't realize it was a secret. Kim always seems to have one of those up her sleeve. It makes me crazy, but I get why she wanted to keep it to herself. That was a messy situation."

"Hopefully, she won't keep any more from you. It was a huge issue in how things played out with Trent and even with the truth about Ava. Kim likes to keep things in for sure."

Our eyes darted toward the back door toward Kim. "Stop talking about me." "Oh, uh, Brian was just telling me how much you loved...What's it called again?"

"Boudain." I helped him out.

"Mmhm. You wanna try some? It's so good."

"What's in it?"

"You've had dirty rice. So, it's something like that but with pork and then it's put into a sausage casing. But when it's smoked, it's heaven." Kim closed her eyes on the last part of her explanation. I was right there with her. Harold always made his from scratch. I'd take a few links for myself and Mom.

Damn, I missed how we used to all hang out here. It was better when Mrs. Duncan had enough of us and retreated to her room. Harold was cool as hell. The four of us would come and chill when he barbecued. We used to play cards and games.

When Kim's brother and sister came with their spouses, we'd have the best time eating the best smoked meats. Mrs. Duncan did her thing with the sides too. Those were the good days when life was simple.

Evan agreed to taste it, and Kim asked how many I wanted to take home. She left to prepare our plates.

"Can I ask you something?" Evan spoke quietly.

I nodded. "Sure, what's up?"

"Kim told me about everything between you and her. But what I don't understand is why. Why did you come on to her if you got a wife?"

Shit. I thought he was asking a general question. Why is this on everybody's mind? Ava was almost two, and I still had to explain.

"Honestly, I don't know what came over me. Over us. It sort of—"

"Alright guys, here's the food. Daddy had a lot of it ready, so these aren't super hot." Kim sat the food down. "Brian, I'm gonna wrap yours up, but here's a piece you can eat now. You need crackers?" She came inside right on time.

"Yes, please," I said.

Evan tensed up again. I doubt that he'd ask me that question in front of Kim so I wouldn't answer it while she was in here.

She came back into the living room and gave me my food in a bag before sitting next to Evan. I put Ava on my lap.

"Be honest," Kim said as she brought a fork of boudain to Evan's lips.

"Mmm! That's delicious, babe."

"Right? Next time, I'll get you some boudain balls. There's actually a gas station that sells them." She laughed, and I guessed why.

Kim thought corner store food was contaminated. Trent and I used to get Mexican or Chinese food at some gas stations, and she'd refuse to eat it. But for those damn boudain balls, she didn't care where they came from.

Kim put some on a saltine cracker and let him eat it her way. She put the plate with only boudain on the coffee table. Evan's held a couple ribs, a chicken thigh, baked beans, and grilled corn. She caught me staring at his plate.

"Don't worry, I put the same thing on yours. The boudain is wrapped separately."

"Thanks, Kim. I appreciate it."

Evan straightened his posture. "You guys act like an old married couple sometimes."

"What?" we said in unison.

"Kim, you're with me. I trust you, but you two can be a bit much."

"Babe, I'm sorry. We've just known each other longer," she explained before kissing him.

Kim turned to me and rolled her eyes so Evan couldn't see her. "Speaking of married couples, how's Denise? I tried reaching out a few times through email. She never responded, but I wanted to tell her how sorry I am for everything."

My jaw dropped. "I never knew that."

"Yeah, Evan convinced me to send the first one. It was hard as hell. Then I felt even more terrible and wrote her again."

"She cried for a while trying to write that first one. It made me realize how bad she felt." Evan grabbed Kim's hand. "That was hard to watch, but I am proud that you did it. Your friend needed that from you whether she answered or not."

Kim's crumbled relationship with Denise never fully crossed my mind either. Damn. They were like Trent and me. Now, nothing. Kim lost her best friend amid all this just like I did.

I was so busy worrying about myself, I didn't realize it hurt Kim to lose Denise too. She never wanted to tell my wife the whole truth because she knew what the aftermath would resemble.

Even when Kim first left, I witnessed my wife spiral after feeling left behind and neglected by the woman who was as close as a sister. Now, Kim went through her version of it.

I filled them in on the lack of progress I'd made with my wife and how she moved back to Houston. Kim was surprised about the move. I forgot to mention that to her the last few times we talked.

Harold walked in on the conversation and gave me the same advice my mom did. Maybe I should listen. Everything was on me, and I couldn't give up so easily even if Denise made it hard.

Evan told us how his wife cheated with a family friend and had the dude's baby. Kim gave me a brief history once before, but he provided details from his perspective. It all made sense why Evan was on edge about me. It's crazy how all of us ended up in each other's lives. There were too many connections.

Evan had the most genuine interpretation of Denise's disconnect. He'd been where she was, but he didn't stay. He shared that his ex-wife didn't fight for him anyway and that she chose the other guy. His advice was to take things slow but not to stop showing up. Kim and Evan were open about their struggles because of our mess.

Suddenly, our conversation halted when we heard keys unlocking the front door. Harold glanced at his watch. "Dammit! She's early."

Kim rolled her eyes. "Brace yourselves."

The door opened. "Harold? Who is that parked in front of the house?" she said locking the door behind her. When she made it into the living room, she found the answer.

"What on God's—what's going on in here?" she asked.

Kim stood up. "Hey, Mom. How was church?" She went in for a hug, but Mrs. Duncan stopped her.

"Diana, please." Harold stared down his wife.

"So, this is how you young folks do it? Just sleep around with everybody and then hang out together."

"Mom! Can you not do this in front of—"

"Oh, please. You are obviously not too proud to have the married man you got pregnant by sitting around with the next guy who might knock you up if he hadn't already."

"Okay, that's enough, Diana. Let's go to the back."

"Harold, if you touch me, you will regret it."

Evan stood up behind Kim. "Um, hi, Mrs. Duncan. I'm Evan Thomas, Kim's boyfriend." He extended his hand, but Mrs. Duncan looked at it with disgust.

"Young man, how are you okay with all this? Do you know that Brian is Ava's father, and he has his own wife? A wife who was Kimberly's best friend. Despicable."

"Yes, ma'am. I'm aware of those things," Evan answered.

Her eyes widened as she placed her hand on her chest. "And you didn't run the other way? You must have a sinful past too, huh?"

Evan shrugged. "Don't we all. That's why Jesus died for—"

"Oh, don't you dare," she snapped at Evan.

My armpits heated like I was next. Didn't she come from church? How was she already fired up? Her spirit should be revived in a good way.

"Why are you doing all of this? I told you I was bringing Evan here to meet you," Kim reminded her.

Mrs. Duncan crossed her arms. "I never understood why. You barely screwed this one not too long ago, and now you are with someone else. When are you going to slow down? You've had enough men already."

"Daddy?" Kim pleaded for him to do something.

All eyes were on this man's low hung head and closed eyes. He let out a long breath and told us to leave. "I cannot believe you're behaving this way," he said to his wife. "We talked about it too many times for you to show out again. You are worse than your mother."

Mrs. Duncan gasped and glowered at her husband.

Evan and I followed Kim through the kitchen then the dining room before finally walking across the front living area. I gave Ava to Evan when we walked outside so I could help

Kim get the car seat from my back seat. "What the hell was that? I knew she gets riled up but damn!"

"She is the main reason I'd rather stay in California. I thought she was tough before, but ever since Ava was born and she found out you were her father, it's been like this."

"Damn. I'm so sorry."

"It's not your fault. Well, not all of it." She tried to muster up a smile.

Harold joined us outside and held Ava. Evan took the car seat from Kim and placed it on the ground. He took her into his arms and held her. As soon as he did, she broke down.

"Baby girl, don't cry," Harold said while Ava laid on his shoulder.

"I'm so sorry, baby. I know that's not what you wanted," Evan told her.

"Why did I expect anything else? She fucking hates me," she got out through the tears.

"Baby girl, your mother doesn't hate you. She's...got—It's complicated," Harold told her. Whatever type of complication that caused a mother to act that way, I wanted no parts of.

Her father gave me Ava and took over with consoling his daughter. Whatever he whispered to her made her cry more. Evan stood nearby with his hands behind his neck. I could tell he was hurting for Kim.

I wished there was something I could do to help. We both did.

CHAPTER
ELEVEN

Denise

I had a busy morning with work. Juggling multiple clients while being the only one here with Layla wore me out. Yesterday, I managed everything perfectly. Then again, most Mondays went smoothly since I usually caught up on things I didn't do over the weekend. Today, I missed my parents' help.

Brian texted me that someone would drop something off at my apartment in a couple of minutes. Just like he said, soon after the message, a guy was at my door holding a Chipotle bag. I accepted the food, and he rushed off.

The perfect burrito bowl with chicken, black beans, veggies, salsa, cheese, guacamole, and sour cream. He even remembered the chips and guacamole on the side for later. This was my exact order every time we ate Chipotle. I didn't have to fight my smile since no one witnessed it. The other container had beans and rice Layla.

I sat on the couch, phone in hand.

Me: Thank you for the food, Brian. I appreciate it.

Lying Asshole: No problem. Anything to help. Hope you enjoy it.

Me: I will. You remembered my order :)

Lying Asshole: I remember everything about you. We haven't been apart that long Denise lol.

Yeah, I guess we haven't. Seeing Brian's saved contact name made me feel bad. I changed it and sat on the floor next to Layla in front of the TV. I ate my burrito bowl in between feeding her the beans and rice. My little bug didn't want to put her stuffed frog down to feed herself. It saved me from peeling smashed beans from the carpet later.

The rest of my workday passed quickly after I put Layla down for her nap. I finished before 3 PM. The sun was out, and the temperature wasn't too bad. I planned to take Layla to the park in the complex in a couple hours. I completed the missed chores from yesterday because I wasn't in the mood then.

We walked to the park, and Layla pointed to the slide. It was too big for her to slide alone so I climbed up with her and we slid down together. After the third time, I took her to the swing. I was already tired.

Brian called and asked if he could come over. He said he was around the corner. Layla would love for her dad to play at the park with her and I could get a break. We hung up after I gave him directions on how to get to us.

When I put in the code to get Brian through the gate, I saw this guy who lived in the building across from me. We always ran into each other. He smiled and waved after the third or fourth time seeing me. He spoke to me at the office once when we were both picking up packages. I didn't remember his name. Whatever it was, he walked straight toward me.

"Well, hello again, beautiful." Damn! He must've came from the gym. He wore a sleeveless shirt revealing his bulging biceps, triceps, and whatever the hell else.

"Who me?" I looked around.

He grinned. "Cute. Who else would I be talking to?"

I shrugged.

"Oh, you thought I was talking to her, huh? She is gorgeous." He said waving at Layla.

"Aww, thank you."

"So, I don't want to sound like I'm watching you or anything, but I never noticed a man with you."

"Yeah. And?"

This guy looked nervous. It was adorable. As fine as he was, nervous didn't seem like something he had to be when approaching a woman.

"You're amazingly beautiful."

"Yeah, you said that."

He chuckled. This would go nowhere, but I needed him to stay long enough for Brian to catch us together.

"Sounds like I'm screwing this up already, huh?"

"I haven't run off yet, so, you're fine." In more ways than one. He looked young as hell though.

"Okay. Um, I was wondering if we could hang out sometime if you aren't tied up with your daughter's father or anything."

I kept pushing Layla who ignored the stranger standing near her mother. "Now, why would you want to do something like that? There are plenty of young ladies out there with no kids you could go after."

"None of them look like you."

"You're right. They look better. And are younger like you. How old are you?"

"Twenty-eight."

"Oh, damn. You look like a baby." He laughed again revealing the cutest smile.

Brian came from the parking lot. He still had on his work clothes. "Hey!"

"Hey, Brian." I sounded a little too cheery.

"What's up?" Brian spoke to my neighbor.

"What's up? I'm Leonard." That's his name? I definitely didn't remember that one. He extended his hand and Brian shook it.

Brian shot a look at me like I should send Leonard away. "I'm Brian, Denise's husband."

"Oh, I didn't—" Leonard tried to get out.

"Don't listen to him. Technically, he's still my husband because technically he slept with my best friend and got her pregnant. We've been separated over a year."

Leonard looked like he wanted to take off running.

"Thank you for your offer, Leonard. I doubt you would be up for this level of drama. I'll see you around."

"Alright, Denise." He looked at Brian. "Good meeting you." Then he walked away.

Brian's head could have exploded. "How was your day?" I asked.

"What was that?"

I took Layla from the swing and handed her to him. "What do you mean? He asked me out before you came over, but I didn't get a chance to answer."

"So, you're just going to play this game with me?"

"What game, Brian? I only told the truth. You standing there like we're some happy family. I bet you assumed buying me lunch would get you in."

"That's not at all what I thought. I wanted to spend time with you and Layla. The food was only food. If it's a problem, I won't do it again."

I felt stupid for a second. His comment about being my husband threw me off, and I did a little too much. I could admit that. Well, not aloud.

"I'm tired. Y'all can stay out here if you want. I'm going inside."

"Am I even allowed to go with you? You never let me come to your place even after all this time."

"You hadn't asked."

"Why would I? You always act like you hate me. I don't want to pressure you."

I rolled my eyes. "Come on. I'm getting hot."

We walked back to my apartment in silence. Brian complimented the decor. He put Layla down, and she ran to the couch to get her toys.

"Dee, what were you doing with that guy?"

"What? He came up and asked if I had a man. He said I was beautiful and wanted to hang out."

Brian's face tightened. "What did you tell him?"

"Why does it matter?"

"You know why it matters."

"If you dare say it's because we're still married. I will remind you that it didn't stop you, now did it?"

He leaned against the nearest wall. After he nodded a few times, he stood up and gave Layla a kiss. "I'll get out of your way."

I said nothing but held his gaze so he'd understand that I didn't care if it upset him. He told us goodbye and left.

Seeing him get a little riled up wasn't as satisfying as I wanted it to be. It was sad and made me regret playing with him. Even if I thought he deserved it.

The next day, I received a package from UPS. Brian bought me a Dooney & Bourke purse. The only person who knew I wanted it was Momma. He didn't warn me about it coming, so I figured yesterday still irritated him.

Me: Thank you for the bag.

???: You deserve it. I won't send anything else. Don't want you thinking I'm tryna buy you. Thought I was being nice. Won't happen again.

Me: I'm sorry about yesterday. I don't know that guy. I am not going out with him.

???: I'm sorry for popping up on you. Your privacy is yours. It's your life.

Me: Brian, don't be like that.

???: You're right. I didn't honor our vows. I shouldn't expect you to. Like you said, we aren't together.

It was true and had been true for so long. But to see his message with the tone I imagined he'd say it, a tear fell. I shouldn't even care. He did so much worse, but I never intended on stooping so low just to get a reaction. It worked better than I wanted.

I called my momma to ask if she talked to Brian. She hadn't. The purse was all his idea. After admitting what I did, Momma said this feeling was what I got for being immature.

"He's trying so hard, Denise. Stop fighting him. You don't think he's been hurting enough over this? Now you're over there behaving like a high school kid."

"Momma, you act like I slept with someone else. It wasn't even that serious."

"Then why are you calling me all upset about it?"

"I don't know. I felt bad. I thought you'd have something helpful to say, not make me feel worse."

"Denise, that's not what I'm trying to do. I only want you to take things serious. This is your marriage you're messing with."

"I'm not the one who...It doesn't even matter. Being here is not like I thought it would be. He tries so hard to be sweet when I know he'd rather curse me out."

"Is that what you want? For him to lose it? Why?"

"It would make it easier to sever all ties. He hasn't changed. Like in a good way. He still cares and still keeps his cool, mostly. Brian isn't making any of this easy."

"Making what easy?"

"Divorce, Momma! I signed this short lease to come here temporarily and prove that I at least tried when we officially call it quits."

"Are you for real? That's why you moved back?"

"Initially, it was for Layla's sake, but it was never for us to get back together. I was warming up to the idea of him. Then this weekend when I dropped Layla off at Debbie's, his other daughter was there."

I didn't tell her about this weekend's mess. The whole thing was still fresh on my heart.

Momma wasn't too happy with how Brian tried to play me, but she still admired him trying to be present in his other kid's life.

To her, many men would forget about the illegitimate child for their wife's sake and then another kid would grow up with issues because of an absent father. Momma had to go all deep on me.

Something switched on. Brian still pursued me. He was a great father to Layla and apparently a great one to his other daughter. How could I hate him for that? The shit still hurt, but I promised myself that I wouldn't be childish about it anymore.

We talked for another half hour before I got off the phone.

Me: I'm sorry for playing with your feelings yesterday. Can you come over for dinner tonight? An apology dinner.

Brian: Thank you for saying that. I can't do it tonight. Hopefully, I'll see Layla at my mom's this weekend. Have a good evening, okay.

Have a good evening? I really hurt his feelings. I'd give him a few days. The next time he did something sweet, I won't fight him.

CHAPTER
TWELVE

Kim

Aunt Vivica took the news of my mom's actions as hard as we did and we were there. She called my dad almost immediately and got loud on the phone about it. She wanted to give him a heads up that she'd call Mom soon to tell her about herself. My aunt had to walk away and finish the conversation in private after she greeted my mother over the phone.

I took Layla out on the balcony, and we drew pictures together. Scribbles mostly, but I'd still display them for her.

Evan convinced me to spend the last two days at his apartment. He wanted to keep me close after the debacle back home. His primary goal was to ensure he would not let my mother deter him from moving forward with me.

I warned him she would not change. That woman turned into a verbally ravaging beast whose sole purpose was to break me down every time she saw me. Daddy couldn't even explain it away like he usually did.

We finally came home this morning, and I let my aunt in on the whole weekend failure. Evan and Trent's scuffle had nothing on the judge trying to scare my man off before insulting him. That ticked Aunt Viv off so much that she put herself in it. She was in the room for a good fifteen minutes before she found us on the balcony.

"I will never understand your mother." She collapsed on one of the lounge chairs.

Sitting back on the couch, I thought of what I'd really done. What was it about me that forced my mom to morph in my presence? Things were messy in my life, yes, but if I could live with it, why couldn't she?

"You and me both, Auntie."

"I will say this. You and your mother have a lot more in common than you know."

"Like what?"

"It's not for me to say. But that woman is on a high horse that no one put her on but herself. It's about time she comes down. God will handle that for sure because she done lost her damn mind." She walked away, saying she was meeting Marissa and her grandkids at the park. I turned down her invitation to tag along.

The only thing I had similar to my mother was part of my DNA, nothing more.

❧❧❧

EVAN'S PARENTS were in town from Arizona. They got in yesterday morning, and he asked me to go with him to pick them up from the airport. I declined.

I drowned myself in enough work to have a valid excuse not to meet his family. I'd seen his mother on his video chats when she called while we were together, but I would only say a few words. The way she looked at me through the phone reminded me of the judge. He dismissed it.

"My mother wants to meet you in person, Kim. You think you can spare a few hours tonight?"

Why did I answer his call? Texting no was easier than

saying it. "I have so many assignments, babe. It doesn't look like I can make it."

"Please? I didn't flake on meeting your family."

"Don't do that, Evan. You remember how that turned out."

"My will not treat you the way..."

"You can say it. The way my mom treated you. I'm sure that's true. I'm just not in the mood."

"But I can get ran up on by your ex?" He laughed, but he was serious.

"I hate you. This is the last time you can use that against me."

"Okay, so that means yes, right?"

"Fine, punk."

"Good. I made reservations at Chez Panisse. I'll be there to get you around six."

"Anything for you, I guess."

"Yeah, after begging."

"Shut up. I'll see you at six."

"I love you."

"Love you too."

Dammit.

ゆゆゆ

THE INITIAL GREETING had me sweating underneath this dress. Everything in me knew she'd be on my ass, but Mrs. Thomas was as sweet and polite as her son. Mr. Thomas was the same. He stood taller than Evan by a few inches. The man aged well and didn't look much older than his son. Besides the grays in his curly hair and goatee, you wouldn't tell he had a son in his thirties.

Mrs. Thomas was gorgeous with a body that competed with mine. Her husband definitely let her know it with those sensual looks he gave her. He kept his hands on her in some kind of way. Now it made sense why Evan did it with me. He learned a lot from his parents. They were acting like kids in love.

Our conversation had gone from my growing up in Houston to what I did for a living, and they seemed interested. Mr. Thomas got a few daring stares from Evan when he mentioned Evan's ex-wife. His father stated his concern that Evan would never trust another woman again. I learned the extent of his depression after everything took place. It was definitely uncomfortable.

"Pops, you don't have to keep bringing her up."

"All I'm saying is that I'm happy you found someone to love again. Because let's face it, you are high in the clouds with this beauty here."

Evan and I locked eyes before he kissed me. "Yeah, I'm up there somewhere. Kim's amazing."

I blushed. "Aww, thank you, baby."

"So, do I hear wedding bells?" Mrs. Thomas sang.

I shook my head. "Oh, no, no, no. Not now. We are still learning each other."

Evan looked surprised. This was not the first time we'd had this conversation.

"Is it because of your baby?" his mother asked. "If so, Evan says nothing but nice things about her. I'm sure being a stepfather isn't an issue."

"Kim wants to take her time, and I agree. It's not that we don't think we're right for each other and it's definitely not about Ava."

"Um, how long will you two be in town?" The faster we could get off the subject the better.

"A few more days. The hotel screwed up our room and comped us two days," his mother answered focusing completely on me.

"Nice," I said.

Mrs. Thomas sipped her wine then kept her eyes on me. "Kim, there is something I've wanted to ask you, and I hope it's not rude."

"If you have to start off with hope, I'm sure it will be. So, please don't." Evan scolded his mother.

She swiped her hand in his direction. "What are your plans with Evan? You have been together for many months. And excuse my bluntness, but my son told me about your scandalous past with the father of your child."

Well, there went the politeness. She sounded excited about a wedding moments ago. It must've been a front. As much as I wanted to put Mrs. Thomas in her place and defend myself, I sat in silence.

"Mom!" Evan placed his hand on top of mine and squeezed it. "You don't have to answer that." He looked at Mrs. Thomas. "I told you not to bring that up."

"That was rude, dear," Mr. Thomas added.

I wanted to get up and leave. I will never live my mistake down. Being honest suddenly felt like the wrong route. No one would know and look at me with disgust in the back of their mind. Yes, I fucked up one time! Why did I always have to answer for it?

His mother's eyes bounced between her husband and son. "Okay, so we are all just going to sit here and act like Kim isn't possibly another Amber. From what you told me, she did the same thing. How am I supposed to feel about that? What if she does it to you? We cannot watch you go through such pain again, son."

Mrs. Thomas lasered on me. "Kim, I don't want to seem like a...bitch, but my son has gone through a lot with that witch that broke his heart. I'll be damned if it happens again."

She stared at her son. "I told you about that girl, but you

just had to marry her hot ass. It would've saved you a lot of grief if you would've only listened to me."

I looked dead into her eyes. "Luckily, you won't have to worry about it any longer. Excuse me."

Evan grabbed my hand when I stood up. "Babe, where are you going?"

"Wherever I can to give your mother some peace or I will end up giving her a piece of my mind. And we don't want that now do we?"

Mrs. Thomas sat back in her chair, mouth slightly ajar.

"Kim, don't leave. She's just trying to look out for me. Rudely, but it's innocent. I promise."

"Evan, I don't need this. Do as your mother wants and find someone with a less *scandalous past*. Did I get that right?" I peered at her, but she looked away.

"I didn't mean to upset you. I only—"

"Meant to piss me off. It worked. Now, both ladies at this table can't be ugly, that would be...should I say...scandalous." I yanked my hand from Evan and darted for the exit.

I couldn't believe I kept my cool. How that woman looked down on me after she excused herself put me in the room with my mother. Ain't no way in hell I'd deal with two judges. Obviously, my mom was ten times worse but judgmental nonetheless.

Outside, I downloaded the Uber app for a ride back home. I didn't have an account and had to set one up. Before I finished, someone snatched my phone from behind me. "What the fuck?" I spun around ready to fight.

Rolling my eyes at his presence, I reached for my phone. Evan put it in his pocket. "Whatever, I'll use the restaurant's phone to call Aunt Viv. I'm going home, Evan. Nothing you can say will make me go back to that table." I walked closer to the curb.

He followed me. "I won't ask you to. Let me take you

home. It's the least I can do. I'm sorry about my mom. She's a little overprotective."

"She has the right to be, but I didn't deserve that."

"No, you didn't and that's why I'm here with you. She will get over it and will apologize to you. My dad will handle her, but I need you to believe that what she said means nothing."

"Scandalous past, huh? Is that how you talk about me to your mother?"

"Hell, no. When I told her about Ava, I had to tell her about Brian. And I'll admit I expressed some doubt I had when I thought he'd try to come between us a while ago. I never thought she'd throw it in your face. She isn't even that type of person."

"Well, I guess I bring out the worst in mothers."

He pulled me close. "Don't say that, Kim." Evan chuckled. "But damn, it seems that way."

"It is so not funny." His stupid grin made me laugh.

"How about you let me make it up to you. Spend the night with me." He planted a kiss on my lips.

"Babe, I have a lot of work to do."

"Shit, so do I. Damage control." He gripped my thigh and pushed his growing erection onto my stomach. His tongue entered my mouth reminding me that I finished my work for the day before his invitation to dinner.

I backed away. "No, I need to go home. Besides, I'm sure your mother wants to protect you from me. Maybe you should let her. I don't know why we try. Our mothers won't accept us."

"You mean to tell me that you'll let what someone else thinks control our relationship. I thought you loved me," he said dramatically.

"You know I do."

"Then why are you trying to throw everything away because of disapproval from people who have no say in what we have. I get that it's stressful but they will get over it or watch us from a distance. We are the only ones that matter. I will say that I'm sorry for how it makes you feel. As for anyone else's opinion..."

He took my hand into his and led us to where he parked. "I do whatever I want and whoever I want. You, my love, are on my to-do list. Stop being stubborn and come with me tonight. Pun absolutely intended." He stepped behind me and pulled my ass into him.

"Does Mrs. Thomas know her precious, innocent son talks like this?"

"There's a lot she doesn't know and has no control over. Especially when it comes to who I fall in love with."

We continued walking with him behind me. "Like your mother said, you should've listened to her then, and you should listen to her now. I don't want to deal with her looking at me sideways for the rest of my life."

"Rest of your life? Was that a proposal? Because my answer is hell yes." He kissed my neck. "I know I said it's early to my parents, but that was just to shut them up. I'm ready. Let's do it."

"Boy, shut up. You know what I mean. I come with so much bullshit residue, and it's not fair you'd have to deal with it from both sides."

"All I care about is dealing with your body from all sides."

"Ugh, I'm serious, Evan!"

"So am I. Ignore the bullshit. The only thing that matters is the three of us. You, me, and Ava. And I guess Brian occasionally." He laughed.

"That's not funny, and it's my point exactly. My baggage." We made it to his car. I turned to face him.

Evan leaned against the car and pulled me between his widened stance. "Babe, if you only knew the half of how you make me feel, then you'd know that I want nothing more than us together. Stop making this more complicated than it has to be."

"Evan, what if—"

"Shut up and let me love you." That tongue of his went hard twirling with mine. Soft bites of my bottom lip and his hand damn near up my dress.

Fine, I'd shut up for now.

CHAPTER THIRTEEN

SOMETHING CHANGED ABOUT DENISE. MY HEART was more than ready for this change, but my mind didn't believe it. Why would she go from hating my existence to suddenly letting me stay at her house for hours? And she didn't leave. She spent the time with Layla and me.

I showed up daily in some way. Whether through gifts, food, or stopping by to help around her apartment. I took her trash out, went to the store with her, and she allowed me to take her and Layla out to eat at least once a week. Denise looked like my wife and acted like my wife before we separated. The wall still stood between us, but it lost a few feet in height over the past weeks.

Mom swore up and down that her prayers had finally been answered and I needed to accept the blessing rather than question it. But Denise could be playing me. Especially since she kept waving at that dude that stayed across from her. He smiled but didn't wave back. If anything had gone on between them, I'd have to accept that too. It wasn't a desirable thought, but if that's what she needed to get back to me, then so be it.

Bath time became my thing. Denise let me come over after

work a few nights to take Layla baths and put her to bed. Tonight was one of those nights.

Denise stayed in her room, and I cleaned my little girl up, read her a story, and tucked her in. After about ten kisses, I pulled myself away so she could go to sleep.

I knocked on Denise's door to let her know to lock up. She opened it, wearing those pajamas I always wanted to rip off of her.

"Hey, I..." I cleared my throat.

That spaghetti strap, skin-tight top and those loose pants that gave her ass room to move freely every step she made took me somewhere else for a few moments. I wondered if she remembered what those did to me.

"You're leaving?"

"Uh, yeah. Layla's down. Thanks again for letting me come over."

"No problem, Brian." Damn, even the way she spoke my name took me to a higher place. "I appreciate you helping out. It means a lot to Layla." She dropped her head. "It means a lot to me too. I know I've been hard to deal with, but you still try, and I appreciate you for it."

I lifted her head with my finger under her chin. She didn't move my hand. My wife let me touch her.

"Dee, there's nothing in this world that'll make me stop loving you. I'm the one who messed up. I only want you to be comfortable with me around. If you never want to get back together, that's on me."

Denise exhaled and leaned against the door frame. "I'm trying to forget the problem. Honestly, I thought I'd move here and prove that you weren't worth my time." She laughed to herself. "But you've been...You've been the same guy I wanted to spend my life with. It's just hard to get over this hump. I am starting to finally see you again. If that makes sense. I can see you more than I see what you did."

Her head lowered again.

All I heard was I still had a chance. A real one. For the first time in almost a year and a half, I had a chance.

"I never thought I'd hear those words from you. I'm here, and I will be here until you're ready. Sleep good tonight, okay?"

"Okay. You too." She followed me to the door.

I turned to face her once we reached it. Her nipples poked through her top. She folded her arms across her chest to cover them. "This may be too soon, but...Can I kiss you? On the cheek, of course."

Denise squinted her eyes while looking into mine. For a few moments, my wife explored my face. She stood on her tip-toes, and I met her lips. The twitch happening in my pants had to keep its distance, but damn it was good to feel her again.

I pulled away so she wouldn't have to. Her eyes were still closed. Then she leveled herself back onto her heels. I wanted to kiss her again, but forcing it would only make her retreat.

The way she looked at me. I recognized that face. She did it every time she contemplated anything. I leaned in boldly and prepared for acceptance or rejection.

Acceptance.

Denise kissed me. More intensely than the soft peck seconds ago. She gently pushed me against the door. Her tongue entered my mouth. I missed out on her sweet taste for far too long. She must've felt my erection. It did what it wanted, tapping her through my jeans. She didn't stop.

Was I dreaming?

I grabbed her ass, and once my hands reached the connection of her back thighs to her behind, I picked her up and wrapped her legs around my waist. I put her against the wall.

Denise stopped kissing me but didn't get down. Her heavy breathing attempted to slow its pace. She stared at me, brooding. I let her stare and spoke not a word. My wife cupped my face with her soft hands and kissed me slowly. After a minute, I tasted her tears.

"Don't cry, Dee," I whispered. "I'm sorry."

I leaned my forehead against hers. "It's okay." I let her down.

Before I could say anything, Layla whined. "Um, let me get her back to sleep. I will see you later."

"Yeah, sure. I love you, Denise."

She paused, gazing at me for a second longer. "I'll see you," I told her to take the pressure off.

When I got to my car, a tear dropped. My wife was coming back to me. Slowly, but still on her way.

Mom almost lost her mind with excitement once I told her what Denise said. The first thing she advised was for me to be consistent but not to push too hard. I'd take this small win and keep chipping away at that wall.

***

I invited Denise and Layla out for a picnic in the park. My plans needed another setting because it poured down as soon as I left Rouxpour with our food.

Denise was at my mom's house dropping Layla off when I called her. Mom didn't tell me her plans when we talked about this picnic attempt a few days ago. I couldn't be mad at her for getting me some alone time with my wife.

Dee mentioned the apartment being a mess, and she didn't want to straighten up. The last option was the home we used to share. When I suggested it, she hesitated. I thought of other places we could go with this food, but after a few moments, she agreed. She'd meet me at our house.

I got home before she did and left the garage door up for her. I scrambled to set up the blanket and food. No time to plate them. The to-go boxes were decent enough. Then I thought of candles. They'd be a nice touch if I could find them. I looked in our closet, the linen closet, and the coat closet. No luck. Denise pulled into the garage.

I met her at the door. "Hey."

"Hey." She walked inside and stood near the dining area where I set the picnic up.

We didn't purchase a formal dining table. The kitchen had a breakfast area that was big enough for the table we had. Since no one ever came to our house for large functions, we didn't see a need for a formal dining setup. We had a couple lounge chairs and bookshelves in that area.

"It looks nice. Clean." She smiled.

"Thanks. Not much has changed. Except for a new TV and game systems."

She burst out laughing. That shit hurt my feelings. Not that I couldn't replace any of it, but damn, she didn't have to destroy my baby. My TV ain't did nothing to nobody. "Sorry about that. Well, not really."

"It's cool. I got your favorite." I pointed at the containers on the floor.

"Wow! You remembered."

"How could I not? When you were pregnant, I spent more time at Rouxpour than anywhere else. They called me by my first name as soon as I stepped in the door."

She found that funny too. Denise was loosening up. Shit! I had nothing to drink besides water and orange juice. I texted my mom to order wine for delivery to my house. She told me about a company that would go to HEB and pick up bottles, then deliver them.

"You wanna eat? I thought we had candles. I wanted to make it all romantic since we didn't have to worry about Layla touching the flames, but I can't find them."

Denise smacked her lips. She walked to the pantry and reached up to grab the candles I thought I searched high and low for.

"Oh."

Her giggles returned. "You've been here alone all this time and still don't know where anything is. Damn shame."

"Looks like I still need you."

She shrugged. "Shall we?"

I lit the candles, and we unboxed the po' boys. She had blackened shrimp. I got fried catfish. Both meals came with a salad. Afterwards, we'd share the bread pudding that thickened Denise up during her pregnancy. She wanted it for every meal of the day.

We talked about old times. Well, the ones that didn't include Kim and Trent. I'd be a complete asshole to bring them up. Many of our memories included those two, and the fact that we were in this position hit me in the chest hard. So stupid.

Denise told so many stories about Layla in the year I missed. I listened to her talk about our little girl and her time in Atlanta. She mentioned her crazy ass cousin, Bam, and how she wanted to hurt me. I wouldn't put it past her to try. She was a rough one. It surprised me that her ass didn't have an assault charge by now.

The doorbell rang. I answered it eagerly. If Denise was this comfortable sober, then she'd have a better time with a little alcohol in her system. That way we'd have something to do after the food ran out. Sip and chat as she used to say.

I poured us each a glass of red wine and sat the bottle between us. The time passed smoothly. Denise's bright eyes lit up the room with every smile, every laugh. Her sexy ass snort even came out whenever she laughed too hard. She always hated it, but I loved everything about her.

We finished the food and sat for about another hour merely talking. Denise left to use our bathroom and took longer than usual. I checked on her and found her in our closet. Some of her things were still there. Actually, a lot of her things were there.

Denise told me about the day she left and how she took only what she needed. The trunk of her car could only fit so much. I found out she stayed at a lot of hotels on her way to her parents. She couldn't stop crying enough to safely drive and didn't want to put Layla in danger. I put her through that.

I apologized, and she stared at me like she did at her apartment. I didn't move in case I read her wrong, but she walked straight over. Her hand trailed from my head to my lips to my neck.

Once on my chest, she gazed into my eyes. Again, she rose to the tips of her toes and kissed me. I pulled her as close as I could. She needed to feel and remember what her touches did to me.

Denise's kisses had the intensity that sent chills throughout every inch of my body. I needed her.

I caressed my wife's entire frame. Her face, her breasts, her ass. She let me. Then I picked her up and sat her on the double vanity.

After one second of hesitation, I went for it. My hands traveled under her shirt and lifted the cup of her bra. Denise's moans returned to my ears. I never thought I'd hear that sound another day in my life. Her eyes closed as I played with her nipple while kissing her soft and slow. She used to love that. Still did.

I unhooked her bra, and her breasts fell from it. They were bigger than I remembered. Fuller. Sexier. I kissed them, holding her tight in my arms as if she'd be taken away from me if I didn't. Her moans grew louder, egging me on to go further.

Pulling her to her feet, I tugged at her jeans. No contest. I unbuttoned and pulled them down enough for the space I needed. Her panties slid with them. I looked at her in the mirror. Her ass also fuller, gave me enough courage to see what she'd allow.

My mouth went back to her breasts while my hand lowered until I found my treasure. Her body shuddered. "Brian," she said just above a whisper. It wasn't the time for her to stop me. My goal was to please her with my touch. So, with my hand, I had my wife winding her hips at the speed of my fingers rubbing her clit and entering her body.

She unraveled in my hands, sounding so damn sexy as she let it out. When she finished, I pulled her pants up myself so she'd understand that it was only about her. Those dazed eyes let me know she wanted me. As much as I could make love to her for weeks straight to catch up for lost time, I wanted to make her wait. It definitely would hurt me more.

Denise kissed me before hooking her bra and putting on her shirt. She walked out of the bathroom blushing away. After a few minutes of making plans for next week, she left with a smile I put on her face.

CHAPTER FOURTEEN

My parents' flight would land in three hours. I cleaned every inch of my apartment. Layla fell asleep right on time for her nap, and I finished my work. If my clients needed me, I'd be available. Otherwise, my weekend was free for Layla's second birthday.

Brian offered to pick my parents up. I let him because I hated driving all the way to Bush Intercontinental. The traffic never ceased on I-45. He wanted to help me with everything lately, and per my mother's advice, I let him.

We spent more time together than I expected. Our proximity played with my mind and my senses. Whenever we're close, I imagined things I didn't want to.

Wanting to be with my husband wasn't the worst thing in the world. Touching him, inhaling him, and hearing his voice all forced me to go back to old feelings. The good ones.

Brian had been the only man since we met about ten years ago and my needs begged for satisfaction. His constant presence didn't help either. Brian would overthink it if we had sex. So would I.

It used to be about trust. My fury toward him blazed

because of betrayal. Brian wasn't a bad guy at all, in fact. But this great and usually faithful man broke my heart and had a child with someone else. How could I live with that? Happily live with it. Not to mention the identity of the mother.

Time flew after Layla woke up. I fed her and watched TV for a while before Brian and my parents stood at my door. They came inside laughing.

After long hugs and a brief tour of my apartment, my parents finally sat down.

"So, we noticed that you don't have much space," Momma stated. "Brian has all that room at the house."

"Momma, I told you I had a two-bedroom. Y'all can stay in my room and I'll sleep with Layla."

Dad turned toward Layla's door. "Where? On the floor?" He laughed.

"They want to take my guest bedroom." Brian somewhat informed me like he feared my reaction.

I should've picked them up my damn self. "How will you get around?"

"We got that taken care of. Brian's gonna take us to rent a car."

My eyes darted at him. "Hey, they asked. What was I supposed to say?" He defended.

"How about no? This makes no sense. Why are y'all changing the plans now?"

"Girl, stop. We can stay where we want and this way you won't have to sleep on the floor," Momma fussed.

"I would really sleep on the couch," I told them. I wanted them to stay with me.

"Hey, if you want us to be together, we can all go to your old house," Dad suggested.

"Oh, hell—I mean, no. We can't all fit there."

"Girl, please. There is plenty of room. Brian already agreed. You and Layla could have his room, we'd have the guest room, and Brian will take his office that has a futon. See? All figured out, and we will be under the same roof."

"Momma, no! We're not doing that. Layla's party will already be at his house." I stood abruptly. Sitting made me feel antsy with all this nonsense thrown at me.

"Exactly! We'll already be there. Besides, Brian's family doesn't know about y'all separating. If we are all there, no one will think anything."

How is that even possible? They never saw Layla until two months ago. In all this time, his people suspected nothing?

With my hands on my hips, I faced that fool. "Brian?"

"Oh, um, yeah. I told my grandmother we had to go to Atlanta for a while. When Stan let me visit, we'd video chat with my mom and grandmother. So, for the party, she and the rest of my family thinks we recently moved back home."

He tightened up expecting me to possibly hit him or curse him out. I should have. I hid nothing from my family about our problems. I didn't want to lie for him to remain the good guy. Why did my parents want to do it?

Dad scooted over on the couch and pulled me down next to him. "Pumpkin, Brian may not completely deserve you doing this for him, but we understand how people can be. He already lost you and Layla for a while. Since they are unaware what happened between you two, it would be awkward for them to find out at Layla's party."

"Denise, I should've told you. Being so busy with you and Layla, I didn't consider my people wanting to be there. My mom mentioned it to one of my aunts, and they made a thing out of it. That's why I asked if we could have a party at my place," Brian admitted.

Momma shifted in her seat. "Is there a park nearby that you can take Layla to? I need to talk to Denise alone."

"Yes. There's one in the complex. I'll take her." Brian walked Layla to her room to get her ready.

"Stan, baby, I need you to go too."

"Okay, sweetheart."

My parents talked about almost missing the flight this morning. Hartsfield-Jackson was a beast, and those two acted slow in crowded places.

Dad, of all people, should have a better sense of direction. It only worked for him in a vehicle. On foot with the pressure of people rushing around him, he lost interest. Then Momma would take the lead, and she didn't do any better.

"We'll be back." Brian carried Layla to the front door.

"I'm coming too." Dad got up and met them at the entryway before leaving.

Momma grabbed my hand. "What's the real problem?"

"It's the same one. I don't want to go along with this little scheme. If you want me to lie for him, fine. Why do we have to spend the night? We will be there before anyone else. You guys staying there is unnecessary. Why would Brian even ask that of you?"

"Well, he didn't. I suggested it."

"The lying part?"

"No, he needs us to back up his story for his people. Staying there would help the story."

"How? What more proof will they need besides what we tell them? They can't be that smart if no one knew Brian was in Houston this whole time."

Most of his family lived on the north side. Some were in Kingwood, and others in the Woodlands. I couldn't wrap my head around them never seeing Brian since I left. Then again, Houston and its surrounding areas was huge, so maybe it was possible if everyone stayed on their sides.

"Don't be rude." Momma swiped my chin. "The truth is... I thought you needed a little nudge in the right direction. Maybe staying there overnight will help you realize that home is where you need to be."

"Oh, come on, Momma. You always take Brian's side."

"His side about what? Y'all fighting again?"

"No, but you keep supporting his needs and force me to go along with anything. What about how I feel?" I hopped from the couch and went into the kitchen.

"Girl, don't get all dramatic. You've been holding out. I talked to Debbie, so don't act like you and Brian aren't good. I know you've been at the house multiple times alone." Her smile made me laugh. She looked like some girlfriend who wanted all the details.

I rolled my eyes. "That means nothing. We only had a picnic and the other times we talked."

"About?" Momma's eager eyes glued to mine.

She wanted my relationship to work more than anyone else. Momma didn't want me to end up bitter like Aunt Rita, who had to basically raised Bam alone because of her ex-husband's infidelity. Brian screwed up once. It was a big fuck up, but not ongoing like Bam's dad. I didn't want that life for myself either.

Brian and I discussed starting over. His first request was for us to live together again. There had to be other steps in between where we were and moving back in. It felt too sudden and too big of a gesture. What if we move too fast?

We were married, but I didn't want to go all in after a couple good months of getting comfortable with each other. I'd been without him this long, how would things be if I needed space?

Having my apartment gave me freedom and independence. I could take care of myself and Layla. As my husband, providing for us was Brian's job. Even though he'd been present and helped me around my house, he felt like he couldn't do his part completely.

I wouldn't let him pay any of my bills. Momma called me crazy for wanting to spend my money when Brian was willing to spend his. She'd never understand. Her marriage was damn near perfect.

After my provider betrayed his duty, being able to do things for myself was me taking my life back. I didn't need him, and I wanted him to understand that.

I explained to my mother everything I felt and admitted to possibly falling for Brian. Because she believed we were heading in the right direction on our own, she dropped the subject. As soon as she asked if we were having sex again, it was time to go. We were not having that conversation. I made her walk with me to the playground.

***

The party was a success. Brian's grandmother bought our story, and I answered most of the questions about life in Atlanta. She had never been past Louisiana, so Georgia seemed like a foreign country.

I told her it was still hot as hell, but the food was better. Then the distracting debate began. We had no more inquiries afterwards.

Debbie had us all over for dinner for my parents' last night. The three of them were all over Brian and me with their ideas of what we should do next. We were friends again. I wanted to take things slow. No one else agreed with my reasoning, but Brian at least pretended to have my back when our parents pushed.

What they saw as inevitable, I viewed as a fifty- fifty chance. I didn't think Brian would ever cross that line again, but he still had to deal with people I wanted nothing to do with. So, I'd hold out as long as I needed to until I could stand the idea of Brian's reality named Ava.

CHAPTER FIFTEEN

Kim

DADDY CAME TO CALIFORNIA THIS WEEKEND FOR A random visit. He told Aunt Viv he wanted a break from Mom, who had started menopause. Daddy ran for the hills before this natural disaster took over my mom. He removed himself to avoid saying something he'd regret. She could've been suffering through this the whole time she was going nuts on us.

I called my mom when he told us about her condition because I wanted her to know that I held nothing she said against her. As a woman who'd eventually have the same experience, I felt awful that he left her. Yes, she was mean before this, but the uptick in her ugly attitude had to be the hormonal changes.

My mother told me she meant every word and how disappointed she was in me for not doing better than she did. Before I could say anything else, she'd hung up.

Daddy said he didn't know what she was talking about when I asked him. Aunt Viv told him to tell the truth. She left us alone with Ava sitting on her grandfather's lap, tapping on his phone screen. She'd mess up his app layout like she did to my phone. He didn't care when I warned him and still let her play with it.

The three of us sat on the barstools at the island while Daddy explained that Mom didn't have the best experiences with Grandma. Because of that, she held me to higher standards.

"Baby girl, you are doing an amazing job with Ava, and I couldn't be more proud of how you are pushing through life without letting the past weigh you down. Everyone does not have that luxury. Your mother is one of those people. She made mistakes when she was younger and refuses to forgive herself."

"What mistakes, Daddy? Aunt Viv mentioned something similar but wouldn't tell me what happened."

Daddy cleared his throat and placed his hand on mine. "Kim, there are things that your mother would have to tell you about her life if she ever can. It's nothing you should concern yourself about, but it affects your mother's ways as of late."

"Why does she only act so off with me? I've never seen her get so mad at Kendrick or Keisha."

"Not to be insensitive, but they'd never been in the situations you have."

"No, Daddy. I'm talking about before Ava. Before Brian and even Trent. As a child and teen, Mom was always harder on me. We never had a real close relationship like other girls with their mothers. It was like that even when I did nothing wrong."

He didn't say anything. Either he wouldn't tell me, or he hadn't noticed it before now. All my life, there was an excuse for her behavior as if I deserved her wrath. I'd learned to live with it and braced myself whenever I felt it coming. Something else caused her issues, and I became the scapegoat.

I noticed that Daddy got uncomfortable, so I dropped it. We talked about Evan once I told him he'd stop by after work.

Those two became buddies. They exchanged numbers months ago. At least one of my parents accepted him.

When Evan arrived, they acted like old friends. The both of them sat outside on the balcony with beers while Aunt Viv and I cooked dinner.

Auntie told me that Daddy talked to her about how he hoped that Evan would be the one to sweep me off my feet. We both knew that already happened and laughed at the idea of Evan officially being a part of the family. He had Daddy's and Aunt Viv's unofficial blessing already.

ρρρ

FAMILY DINNER WAS every other Saturday night since Sundays were reserved for immediate family time at my cousins' houses. Last Sunday, Evan joined Aunt Viv and me after church. He raved about her meatloaf and mentioned how he made a sweet sauce to top his.

Auntie declared that anything sweet with meatloaf other than a side of yams was wrong. When I vouched for it, she had to find out for herself if Evan could burn in the kitchen. So, he agreed to cook not only for her but for everyone the following week.

Daddy's visit fell on the perfect weekend because he could also be a witness of Evan's greatness. I was the sous-chef and server. He'd been prepping for about an hour before the loves of Aunt Viv's life, Malik and Cory, arrived with their families. The guys clowned my baby for his denim camouflage apron and chef hat. I loved it when he wore it. Mostly because I bought it for his birthday.

One thing Evan would always say was that no one could see him in the kitchen. As much as I wanted to claim myself or even Daddy for being a better cook, it would be a flat out lie.

Evan was the legit. His mother did a great job training him

to throw down. He didn't follow recipes; he got creative and put his twist on almost everything.

So, for Evan's birthday, I found the apron and hat then had "Y'all Can't See Me" embroidered on it. He almost fell over laughing when he saw it. He'd worn it in the kitchen ever since. Today was no exception.

Evan planned this meal like he'd get paid. He put together a salad with fresh tomatoes, avocado, bacon, and sautéed shrimp on top of chopped greens. My baby even made his own vinaigrette.

I served everyone at the table, and once I set the plates in front of Malik and Cory, envy settled in. They looked around as if they weren't impressed. However, both cleaned their plates ahead of the ladies and even my dad.

While everyone else was busy with the salad, Evan pulled bacon-wrapped stuffed shrimp from the oven. He took note that Aunt Vivica loved shrimp about as much as I did. He promised to make her favorite appetizer and delivered.

After placing each piece on a platter and saving a few for Evan and myself, I sat it in the middle of the dining table. The women gasped.

"Bro, why are you showing off?" Cory asked my man who slightly smiled.

Evan rested on the island for a moment. "I'm giving the beautiful ladies what they want. Your mother requested this dish."

"Yes, I did! Mmm-mmm!" was all Aunt Viv could say as she stuffed her mouth.

"Don't worry cousins, I'm sure Evan can give you some tips." I winked at both men.

"Please do," Tara quickly begged, teased her husband. Malik scowled at her before nodding like he'd remember that.

"Yeah, please," Marissa seconded, chuckling. Cory pressed his lips together, knowing they could use a tip or two.

"Okay, okay. Y'all need to chill. It's good, but y'all being extra," Malik told the women.

"We ain't doing enough. We're trying not to hurt your feelings," Aunt Viv said.

Daddy cracked up at his nephews' whining. The guys cooked occasionally. This is not the first time the women had dinner catered without having to do anything but eat.

However, Evan was in the zone whenever he found himself in a kitchen. For the short time I'd known him, this was nothing. He cooked for me more often than we ate out. It was a high for him to create a dish that made someone close their eyes and savor his hard work.

Malik and Cory never received that amount of gratification for their efforts, and I saw that it damaged their egos. Their mother and wives were enjoying the food way too much for the men's comfort.

"I'm ready to go," Malik stated. "If the main dish is better than this, I'm gon' to have to excuse myself and cry in the corner."

We all laughed. Malik looked serious, but savored the shrimp as much as the ladies.

I walked over to Evan who wore the sexiest smile watching me. "You are killing it, babe."

"So, are you. That chef's hat may have to make its way to the bedroom," he whispered.

"You better stop," I said before kissing him.

"You stop," he whispered between kisses.

"Ewww!" a few of the kids whined.

"Okay, lovebirds. We're happy for you and all, but you better not burn our food because you can't keep your hands off each other," Aunt Viv warned.

I turned around and scrunched my face at her. "We got this."

Minutes later, I plated the medium rare steaks with a

creamy garlic sauce topped with none other than three jumbo blackened shrimp. Then I added the roasted asparagus and parmesan crusted potatoes. Mouth salivating as I finished the last plate.

Aunt Viv received her masterpiece first. "Oh! Honey, when are you going to marry him? Your auntie can get used to this."

"I'm working on it," Evan answered.

"Ha! Yeah right. It's too early for all that." I felt his eyes on me but I didn't face him.

"How long has it been?" Tara asked.

"Ten of the most amazing months of my life," Evan answered from the kitchen again.

"Awww, how sweet! It hasn't been a year yet?" Marissa chimed in.

"Nope. It'll officially be a year right after Ava's birthday. It seems like forever already," I told her.

"It could be." Daddy winked at the chef.

I narrowed my eyes at Evan. He went back to serving the kids the baked chicken strips, mac and cheese, and roasted broccoli.

Evan mentioned marriage multiple times before to learn my views in general. It was definitely a step I'd love to take one day, but I needed to shake off the remnants of my past. I trusted Evan because he earned it, but my mistakes still carried a weight I wasn't sure he'd be ready to take on full-time.

Between our mothers, my baggage and his, I didn't know how far this would go. I loved him enough to find out, but we had a lot to deal with.

After dinner ended, Evan and I cleaned up before he had to go home. Everyone else stayed so the kids could play and the parents could chill.

"That was too good, girl. He is definitely a keeper," Aunt Vivica suggested as she stretched out on the couch.

"I wish Malik knew his way around the kitchen like Evan," Tara teased as her husband sat next to her rubbing his belly.

"I was thinking the same thing about my wife," Malik countered.

Everyone laughed at those two knowing Malik had every right to wish. Tara wasn't a horrible cook. She needed time to grasp her way around the kitchen with more elaborate meals. Malik could survive on spaghetti and store-bought rotisserie chicken for a little while longer.

ᑭᑭᑭ

DADDY'S FLIGHT was scheduled to depart tonight. The four-day escape came to an end. Before he got on a plane, I had to press for answers.

My father swore up and down I shouldn't worry about my mom's issues with me because they didn't exist. Aunt Viv got on him about Mom's craziness one more time. She knew what no one would tell me.

"Y'all are just as bad as her." Both of them gave me a look like I had cussed them out. "All these years, she's been tripping on me, and you both know why. Talk to me. Plus, if it's not about me like you said, Daddy, then help me understand."

Aunt Viv glanced at my dad in a way that felt like she thought I should know whatever it was. My father took a deep breath and said nothing for a minute.

"Baby girl, with everything in me, I believe that her issues are hers to bear. She wants better for your life, and it makes her go off the hinges because of the turns your life has taken. It's hard to understand, I know. But she loves you."

I looked away and rolled my eyes. "So, that means no one will tell me the truth. I already know about Mom not being married when she had Kendrick."

"Yes, that's true. Now, you have a daughter with a man

116

that wasn't your husband. See how that makes her feel like she didn't accomplish what she wanted for you?

I shrugged. "All I know is that my life is an embarrassment to her. It hurts that my own mother can't accept me. So what if I messed up? No mother who claims to love her children treats them like she treats me. It doesn't add up."

Those two focused on each other like they had telepathy. Something was up. "Whatever, y'all. I'll just continue being the prodigal child that won't make it back home because my mother doesn't want me. Even *that* dude's family welcomed him with opened arms."

"I'm sorry, baby girl. I used to think she'd come around, but now I can't even say when."

"Thanks, Daddy. It's not your fault. We will see how much she'll allow herself to miss out on because she won't love me unconditionally. And don't say she does. Your wife's love comes with harsh conditions. I'm done with it."

We dispersed around the house. Daddy took Ava to the balcony. I called Evan to let out my frustration. He couldn't do anything but listen. When I was done venting, I apologized to Daddy for pushing him about that woman.

He encouraged me to keep doing what I was doing for myself and Ava and focus on my relationship with Evan. Daddy mentioned that he was ready to walk me down the aisle and had a feeling that Evan might be the one he'd lead me toward.

All this talk about marriage scared me. Was I wife material? Evan and I haven't even made it to a year yet.

After Daddy left, Aunt Viv got ready for her date tonight. Out of all the people we thought she'd be a good match with; she met a nice-looking man at Tara's daycare.

Tara invited her to Grandparents Day, and another kid's grandfather introduced himself. Weeks later, she picked the boys up since they were spending the weekend with us. The guy was there and asked for her number.

Mr. Darrin Brown took my aunt out five times in two weeks. She enjoyed his company, and I loved hearing her gush over him. She doesn't have faith that she'd fall in love, but he definitely put a smile on her face for the time being. If anyone deserved happiness in the romance department, Aunt Viv did.

CHAPTER
SIXTEEN

Kim got in yesterday morning with Ava, Vivica, and Evan. It's been months since their last visit. I usually saw Ava more often, but with Denise being here, I couldn't leave. Kim understood my need to stay home and did more video chats so I could at least see Ava.

We all had lunch at my mom's house. She was so excited to see Vivica. They ditched us to go hang out and catch up. Kim and Evan went shopping for decorations. Kim's sister-in-law, Tina, made professional-grade cakes on the side and would make Ava's birthday cake.

Baby girl and I had grocery duty. Basically, I had to pick up the groceries from Sam's Club in two hours. Not too bad.

Since I had time to burn, I asked Denise if I could stop by. She agreed. I had a feeling she'd slap me when I showed up.

At the door, I took a deep breath and knocked. When she opened it, her head tilted sideways. "Really, Brian?"

"Let me explain."

Layla came around the corner and squealed at Ava's presence. It shocked the both of us. Ava wanted to get down to get to her. They were too little to remember each other, and they'd only spent a short time together.

"I guess I have no choice. Come in." I kissed her cheek on the way inside.

We sat on the couch after she asked me to help her bring this ball pin into the living room for the girls to play in.

"Look at them." Denise's eyes were glued on the girls.

"It's crazy to see them together like this. How do you feel about it?" I only asked because the last time my daughters were in the same room, my wife lost it.

"Brian, I won't lie and say it's all good, but she *is* your daughter. If I will ever be able to forgive you, I have to somehow accept her."

The room filled with giggles and brief words between the girls. Ava kept repeating, "Ball!" Sometimes it sounded like a statement and then a question.

Layla placed the balls on top of the inflatable and watched them twist and turn all the way to the bottom. Every time the ball mixed in with the others in the pool part, Ava grabbed it and handed the ball to Layla for a repeat.

"She's beautiful, Brian. She looks so much like Layla."

"I got strong genes, I guess."

"Yeah, let's hope it stays that way. The more she looks like you, the better. I can stomach it a bit more."

I understood why. Not that I had any control on whether she'd ever favor Kim over me. I prayed that she doesn't, only to make it easier on Denise.

She broke away from watching the girls and turned my way. "You hungry?"

"No, I'm good."

"Eat, eat!" Layla chimed before walking toward the pantry, pulling at the knob.

I chuckled when Ava mimicked Layla after following her to the kitchen. "Well, it looks like they are."

"Okay, then. Is Ava allergic to anything?" Denise rose from the couch.

"Damn, I don't even know."

"Please find out. We don't need nothing dangerous happening."

I took her hand into mine before she headed to the kitchen. She loosened up, and I pulled her into me, gazing into her eyes. "I love you, Denise. You are amazing. I don't deserve you."

"You got that right. And you don't have me." She nudged my chest before I kissed her. Denise melted in my arms like she used to.

"Yet," I informed her.

She rolled her eyes, giving me one more kiss and then I let her go. I texted Kim to find out about any allergies. We got the okay to give Ava anything.

For an hour and a half, I had my whole family together. Life couldn't get any better.

On my way out, I asked Denise to think about allowing me to bring Layla to Ava's birthday party. When it initially came up, her body tensed, and I stopped pushing. Since the party was the next day, time had run out. I wanted both girls there.

"We'll see, Brian."

Any answer trumped the usual flat out no.

ɲɲɲ

KIM and her crew arrived early in the morning to make the food and decorate. Kim let Ava sleep over with me last night. When I got to my mom's, the food almost took me out. It was all Evan's doing. He cooked breakfast and had my mom in love.

Vivica repeated to Mom, "I told you."

I couldn't get mad at him. He came with his A- game and not simple eggs and bacon. Dude showed out with homemade biscuits, candied bacon, scrambled eggs with spinach and some type of cheese, and grits.

Kim couldn't wipe the smile off her face once I admitted he exceeded my expectations and skills. She told him to go all out for us. He did.

The doctor gained points with me and apparently all the women. There wasn't much to hate him for once he made my mom fall for him.

Hours later, the party was in full swing with Ava running around my mom's house with her cousins. I picked up Layla before our guests trickled in. All of Kim's immediate family attended except Mrs. Duncan. We all agreed that she needed to sit this one out. I doubt she would've come anyway.

Mom, Vivica, and Evan were in the kitchen cooking and handing out platters of food they prepared together. Kim ran the party with games for the kids. Layla loved being around other children. Harold and Kim's siblings were having a good time.

I went back and forth with Denise through text since she had second thoughts about Layla being around Kim's family. I assured her everything was okay. I sent pictures of Layla playing with the kids while making sure Kim was out of frame. She couldn't take it and texted that she was on her way.

Kim knew something was up and when I let her in on the issue, she told me to go to Denise. She didn't want my wife upset with no one there for her. Mom and Kim made me leave Layla.

Kim apologized for the strain this put on my progress. I didn't want to leave the party, but she insisted and reminded me of the many birthdays ahead that Ava would actually remember.

Once I stepped outside, Denise pulled up. I convinced her to let me use her car and drive to my house to talk. It took a minute because she wanted Layla out of the house. She stared out the window in silence the whole ride.

At my house, I talked her into coming inside. "Nothing will happen to Layla, Denise. My mom is with her. You trust my mom, don't you?"

Denise finally got out of the car. Inside, I led her to the couch so she could get everything out. She paced the floor while speaking on what sounded like every thought that came up. It was nothing I hadn't already heard. After talking about Kim being around Layla, I told her to trust me, and she eventually loosened her grip on the matter.

I brought up her moving back in with me so she would see that she had nothing to trip about. I belonged to her and wanted to take care of my family completely. She wouldn't give me any hint on whether she'd thought about it and usually used Layla as an excuse to change the subject. Even now, she wouldn't give me an answer.

"Do you know how much I love you? I want you to be happy. Although our family is complicated, we can make it work. You believe me, right?"

"I don't know, Brian. It's too much."

"It can be, but that's what I'm here for. Let me be there for you. You won't have to think twice about anything. I won't let anything bad happen. And I will never hurt you again. This is on me. Your discomfort is on me. But everything is good, okay?"

Denise had worry written all over her face. I wanted to show her she had no reason to be. All she needed to feel was the love I had for her.

I held her close and lifted her chin. "Please forgive me. I will never hurt you again."

My lips brushed against hers, and those tears of hers came down. "I love you," she whispered.

I fought like hell not to cry my damn self. With everything we'd gone through and the past months of us getting here, I still didn't know if I'd hear her say those words.

Denise pressed her lips onto mine softly. After a few pecks, I slipped her my tongue, and we kissed her tears away. All that was left were her quiet moans and long gazes whenever she pulled her lips from mine.

"I want you. All of you," I admitted as if she didn't know.

She stepped back, never breaking away from my eyes. I tugged at the hem of her shirt to pull her toward me. "Come here." I led the way to our bedroom, and she willingly followed.

Once near the bed, I sat on the edge as she stood firm in front of me.

"Babe, relax. It's only me." I grabbed at her once more, and she finally moved her feet.

Making her straddle me, Denise stared into my eyes. Her gaze searched for something. "What is it? You don't want to do this?" I asked.

She rested her palms on my shoulders. "I don't know what I want, Brian."

"Okay. We can stop. The last thing I need is for you to feel uncomfortable. Just know that I love you and always will. If I have to wait longer, then that's what I'll do."

Her eyes moistened. Almost sparkled. Denise leaned in closer to my face until I felt those soft lips. This time, her kiss felt unsure, even timid.

"You promise you haven't been with anyone else." Our foreheads now connected to possibly avoid eye contact on her end. Being that she'd asked me the same question multiple times, she still had to hear my answer. If I had to answer it every damn day, I would. Whatever made her feel safe.

"Dee, you are the last woman I'd made love to, and I want to keep it that way for the rest of my life. As hard as it may be, I need you to trust me."

She backed her head away but stayed seated on my lap. "Brian, I can't move back in here."

"Why not? I told you I'd sleep in my office until you were ready to share our bed."

The right corner of her mouth rose as she contemplated my offer. "You know why."

I did. Still, Denise knew my relationship with Ava wouldn't change. She was a part of my life and would be in this house whenever her mother allowed. Kim had not come here in a couple of years. Her guilt was as deep as mine, and she didn't feel right even coming to our neighborhood.

"I love you, and I want you to be happy. Especially since I took that away from you in the worst way. Whatever you need, I got you. But understand that I cannot turn my daughter away. I need you *and* my girls."

She barely rolled her eyes and pushed out a long breath. "I want to trust you. I do. It will take time. We can't jump back into the swing of things. Everything is so different now."

"Not everything." I lifted my hips so she could feel my growth beneath her.

"Be serious, Brian. This is not a trivial thing. You have another child by..."

"Okay. Okay. I get it. Like I said, I will wait on you."

I placed my hand on the side of her face. She closed her eyes and let it rest there. When I saw my opportunity to finish what we started, I drew closer and kissed her. Her body relaxed.

Placing my free hand on the small of her back, I pulled her as close as she could get. My dick jumped again. Denise's tongue met mine and did the same dance as if they never stopped. I missed her warm tongue and the comfort of her closed eyes as she melted in my arms.

"Mmm," she moaned, giving me the motivation I desired to finally end this torturous era in our lives.

I grabbed a handful of her ass in each palm spreading her cheeks, feeling the fullness. As much as she complained about putting on a little weight, I appreciated the extra plumpness to grab onto. Denise was always gorgeous and so sexy, but these added curves did something to me.

"Can I make love to you?" I whispered between kisses.

Her eyes met mine, sparkling. She exhaled and nodded.

Yes? Yes! Yes.

Immediately, I stood up while holding her. I gently rested her sexy ass body onto our bed. *Our bed*. With no more pausing or guessing, I removed her jeans and panties together.

My wife sat up and yanked at my pants before pulling them down. Once my fully hard flesh was free, it flung up and down from the release of the elastic waistband of my boxers. She grabbed it and stroked my shaft never looking away. It was like she reminisced on what it used to do to her.

She looked up at me, locking eyes until she placed gentle kisses all over it. Every connection sent waves through me. This moment was about my wife and how I needed to make her feel comfortable with me. As hard of a decision it proved to be, I had to pull away from those hungry eyes so I could service my wife the way she deserved.

"Let me take care of you, okay?"

Denise nodded with her eyes shut as she lay back, ready. Ready for me to do whatever.

I traced my fingertips from her knee to her thigh to her exposed belly button. She breathed deep, slow breaths, still awaiting anything. What the fuck did I think when I betrayed this woman that lay before me? It was the dumbest thing I'd ever done.

Her body shivered beneath my touches, and all I could do was look at her. Once her eyes opened, it meant she'd been waiting long enough.

Dropping to my knees, I kissed her exposed thighs while gazing at the glory between them. The one place that once called on me constantly. The one place I'd taken for granted. The one place I'd been banned from coming near for too damn long.

Denise squirmed around the closer I got to my obvious destination. As much as my body wanted to be inside hers, I chose patience. My hand slowly rubbed near her belly button before the other joined that area, grabbing onto her waist and pulling her closer to the edge of the bed.

Her moans were subtle and quiet. I kissed the lips closest to me. Denise quivered at the smallest touch. I rested the tip of my nose right above her love, inhaling all of her. Breathing her essence. I kissed her labia soft and slow as if they were the same lips on her beautiful face.

Closing my eyes, reacquainting myself with my favorite place, I slid my tongue inside my wife. Her thighs were now closer to my ears. That's when I had to give her everything I had. Licking, sucking, and pushing inside her wetness.

I tucked my shoulders below her thighs lifting them up slightly to get closer. Nibbling on her clit as her moans turned into yelps and eventually screams.

I fluttered my tongue on her sweet, sensitive spot. Savoring every drip of her as she climaxed, yet still going. Tugging on every part of her I could, slurping the excess juices rushing from her body.

"Aaahhh!" she let out in a way that had my dick throbbing. I got so lost in her that I never saw her post up on her elbows. I didn't feel her eyes on me as I licked her clean.

Her moans calmed down as her breathing tried to do the same. "Shit, Brian!" Her body continued to jerk.

"I told you I missed you."

She dropped her head back. "Dammit, boy," she breathed out.

If this were the last time I had to prove to my wife I needed her back, I would hold nothing from her.

CHAPTER SEVENTEEN

I slowed my breathing to relax. How did we get here? Not complaining, but from what he my body, there was no turning back. No going without it again. Was I ready? To feel this feeling physically? Hell, yes. But everything that came with it? I didn't know.

My mind and body were at odds. My heart was somewhere in between. Brian stood up baring it all, waiting for permission to give me more of him. He'd most likely stay there until I admitted I wanted him. I nudged the back of his thigh with my foot for confirmation.

His tongue lit a fire only he could put out.

Brian hovered over me, taking me all in. I did the same. My husband was real again. I broke from his gaze and glimpsed at his pectorals that were more defined than I remembered. When I touched them, rubbing my fingers from one to the other, he closed his eyes. His dick tapped my leg with every movement my fingers made.

I raised my knees and spread my legs apart. Brian's head dropped lower until our foreheads met. I knew what he thought, what he felt. The same emotions ran through my body and mind. "It's okay." I kissed his lips. This was real.

Every kiss, every touch slowed time. We were husband and wife as if nothing ever came between that realization. Brian caressed my clit causing me to jerk beneath him. Then he guided himself into my body. I held my breath a few seconds to let this moment sink in. He began with slow strokes like our bodies needed to adjust to one another.

Brian's head dropped once more, and our cheeks touched as he pushed himself deeper. My moans in his ear were always a weakness, but I couldn't hold them back. Brian had the perfect size for my body until it wasn't. Sometimes he'd hit a spot that convinced me his dick grew.

When he pushed and pulled himself in and out faster, I screamed. He found my special spot too soon, and I held him back to stop moving as my body quaked for at least half a minute.

I opened my eyes once it ended. Brian wore this sexy smirk at my second orgasm. With two out of the way, Brian took complete control. He pulled out and turned me around, bent me over and entered me from behind. I screamed worse than before, I could feel every single part of him.

Whenever he felt himself reaching his peak, he'd tell me to hold on. He wanted to last as long as possible. I loved it when he used to do that. It showed me how much he wanted to please me to the max before he got his. That's precisely what he did.

Two positions later, I took the lead and got him on his back. Watching my husband's closed eyes, lip- biting, and his hands going back and forth from his head and to my hips made me lose it. He fought hard to keep himself together, but as I rode him faster and harder, he didn't stand a chance and neither did I.

His moans and grunts between soft grips of my breasts,

my waist, and my hips caused our final explosion. He took over and held on to my waist while driving himself upward with powerful thrusts until he froze and released all that he had inside me. I felt the heated burst within my walls while violently trembling my damn self.

I sat on top of him as he caressed my naked body. We said nothing and let our eyes explore each other. Once I got off, the mess we made dripped from me. Brian got towels from the bathroom. After we cleaned up, I laid in his arms in silence.

Minutes later, we heard his phone from the living room. He kissed my forehead and answered it after I told him it might be Debbie. I heard him say we were okay and would be there in a bit.

"The party's over. Everyone is leaving my mom's house. We can wait a little to make sure everyone left."

"Okay."

Brian sat on the bed. "Dee, I know this doesn't mean we are back together, but—"

"Let's not talk about anything serious. I'm still trying to catch my breath. You wore me out."

He chuckled. "Good. It took everything in me not to have you pissed at me for coming too soon."

I laughed at his face. He appeared relieved that he accomplished that much. "You did your thing. Now, I need a shower."

"Go right ahead. I'll get in after you."

"I don't have any...Oh, yeah." Brian pointed to my untouched panty drawer. "I keep forgetting about that."

"I'll call my mom and see how everything went."

I stood from the bed and walked to the bathroom while he threw on some sweatpants. "Hey, could you not tell your mom about this? We don't—"

"Dee, I do not talk to my mom about stuff like this. I got you. It's our little secret." He had already made it to the door next to me. He leaned in and kissed my forehead then my lips. What was I going to do with him?

ᵽᵽᵽ

AFTER AVA'S PARTY, life returned to normal. Brian still came to my apartment to put Layla to bed multiple times a week. The only difference was that each time we spent the night in my bed.

Adding sex to the equation did not help me see anything besides wanting him inside me wherever I laid eyes on him. It became so distracting that one time I put Layla in her high chair in front of the TV so she'd be secure while I took Brian to my room and relieved all my backed up sexual frustration.

We couldn't make love enough. My ass acted like a damn virgin who had sex for the first time and couldn't stop. Brian always had me head over heels in bed, but this reintroduction to ecstasy took over me. By the third week, we damn near lived together since he'd leave in the mornings.

Eventually, he asked us to spend nights at the house so he wouldn't have to drive home to get ready for work. He claimed that he didn't want to bring clothes whenever he came to my place. He thought it would be presumptuous to bring a bag each time.

The first night at the house, he picked up Rouxpour for dinner. After we ate, he led me to the guest bedroom where Layla would sleep.

When we walked into the room, I couldn't believe my eyes. He painted the walls purple and pink with huge butter-flies on the side where a canopy bed's headboard was set up.

There was a princess trunk filled with toys and a white dresser tucked into the closet. He mounted a small TV on the wall near the corner next to the window covered with pink and purple sheer curtains.

"When did you do all of this?"

Layla used the step stool to get into the twin bed. Brian stayed close to her in case she fell. "I painted it last year, but I slowly bought the furniture hoping one day she'd have this room. Mom helped me out obviously. It's been finished for months."

"How have I not seen this until now?" I walked around touching the walls and the little furniture. Layla pointed to the small table with a tea set, still in the package, sitting on top.

"Whenever you were here, we were busy doing something else or talking. Layla saw it before."

"It's beautiful, but the bed might be too big for her."

"Oh, yeah." He brought a box down from the top shelf in the closet. "I will put on these side rails so she won't fall."

"Hmm. Looks like you thought of everything. I love it. You did good."

He smiled. "Thanks, beautiful."

We walked into the living room after he grabbed a few toys. Layla ran around the place like it was home. Brian took my hand and led me to the couch to sit. "This past month has been the best one of my life."

My cheeks heated. "Mine too."

"So, why won't you move in with me? Before you mention you already renewed the lease, I will pay for any fees to break it. We don't have to live apart anymore."

"Brian, being with you feels right. I won't lie about that, but..."

"But what, Denise? What are we doing here if we aren't trying to move forward? I want you and only you. Haven't I shown you that much?"

I dropped my head. "You have."

Brian showed up and made everything sound good. However, I could not discern whether my feelings toward him stemmed from all the sex or if I truly loved him. Those three words came out my mouth last month, but not since then. It confused the hell out of me.

"Baby, I know it's been crazy what we've been through. Trust me, I get it. But it's crazier that you and Layla have to live in that apartment when I'm right here. We've been spending so much time together anyway."

"Okay, give me a week."

He narrowed his eyes. "For?"

"I need to see if I'm ready. You can't come over. We cannot sleep together. Let me think about it, okay?"

He exhaled into his fist. "If that's what you need to do, I'm all for it. Just don't think too hard."

Together we got Layla ready for bed and read her a story from the collection Brian had on the bookshelf beneath the mounted TV.

Once we changed clothes and got in bed, I already knew my answer.

CHAPTER
EIGHTEEN

Our first anniversary came and went with no luxurious celebration. Ava caught a bug that eventually infected us all.

We knew she was sick the night before our anniversary. Evan previously got us reservations for that night, and the three of us would spend the weekend out of town.

When our plans changed, he had us over so he could help me with Ava. Aunt Vivica had already caught it, or maybe she was the one who spread the sickness.

Instead of a restaurant, Evan cooked our favorite. Smothered pork chops, roasted veggies, and potatoes. He prepared the same meal the first time we had dinner at his place.

I didn't get him anything. Work backed up on me, and I spent the last couple of weeks cramming. Any free time I had, he wanted me with him and left me with no time to shop.

After dinner, we chilled on the couch in the living room where my gifts were. I reached for the wrapped box sitting next to the bag on his coffee table. Evan almost knocked me over snatching it from me. He explained that he only had the box out to remind himself to return it. It was covered with floral paper and the size of a shoe box, so I asked to still see it. He refused and pushed the other gift my way.

The bag was full of items I kept saying I'd get myself but hadn't. I didn't realize how much I mentioned the *Martin* hoodie I saw online, or the cute date games always advertised on social media that Black people created. Evan listened and made me feel special. I made up for my lack of gifts in the bedroom.

By the end of the next day, we caught the bug. After it cleared, we *Lysol*ed the hell out of Aunt Viv's house and Evan's apartment.

To make up for our anniversary, he booked us a five-day trip to Miami after the holidays. I had never been that far from Ava. Aunt Vivica pushed me to have fun. I caved to shut her up.

In Miami at the Marriott Stanton hotel, we were right on South Beach with the view to prove it. The sun beamed on parts of my skin that had gotten little exposure otherwise. I dressed for the weather and to catch Evan's eyes. Since he always complimented my body, I showed it off.

The first night was a make-up night. We stayed in bed until the following afternoon. I didn't remember the last time I got a decent amount of sleep. Well, whenever we slept. Evan was on a mission to put on a marathon or something. He tore my ass up.

The second day we spent all day on the beach and ate at a few spots on South Beach's strip. Evan took so many pictures of me in the water, a stranger would think I paid him. He claimed I didn't have enough pictures of myself.

Day three, we chilled on the beach again but did a little shopping before Evan asked if I wanted to hit a club. Why not? We couldn't come to Miami and not go to at least one club.

At STORY Nightclub, the music blasted through the

speakers and drove the girls wild. I guess the experience justi-fied the high ass admission. Asses shaking everywhere with men leaning their pelvises near the closest one. I had two drinks before gaining the guts to dance.

Evan was too cool and sexy on the floor. I did most of the sweating. He held onto my waist ensuring I felt what my grinding did to his body.

Whenever I stood straight, he planted kisses on my neck, causing me to bend over again and wind my ass onto him. Clubs weren't my thing, but anywhere with Evan was where I wanted to be. Feeling his hands all over me in a public place and dancing like no one saw us gave me a new high.

We took a bathroom break. With perfect timing and only a few women waiting, I finished first. So, I waited for him at the bar after getting a bottle of water.

Some guy stood a little too close and leaned in even more. "What you doing ordering water? Still uptight, huh?"

I turned ready to politely tell this dude he had the wrong woman. He must've thought he knew me. My eyes widened at the familiar face. "Oh my goodness!" We laughed. "How are you?!" I hugged my puppy love ex from high school, Rashaad.

"Good, baby. Real good." He grabbed me again to face me. We stood at enough distance for him to check me out. "Damn, you looking all scrumptious."

"Boy, shut up. You don't look bad yourself. I haven't seen you in over a decade."

"I refused to move back home after college. I couldn't. I fell in love with this city."

"Cool. It's so good seeing you. I can't believe you don't have a beer gut." I playfully hit his abs popping through his too-tight shirt. "You definitely didn't have these."

He chuckled. "I could say the same about you. You got a little junk back there." Rashaad glanced at my ass before placing his hand on the small of my back.

I felt a swipe from behind before someone pulled me backward. "What are you doing?" Evan asked me but kept his eyes on Rashaad.

"This you?" Rashaad narrowed his eyes at Evan.

"Yes, this is my boyfriend, Evan. Evan this is an old high school friend, Rashaad. Everything is cool, Evan." I attempted to bring him down from wherever he'd gone. Evan had that look in his eyes like he did with Trent.

"What's up, man?" Rashaad spoke to Evan, who only nodded at my ex.

"Nice seeing you again, Kay. Hope to see you another time. We can catch up later, a'ight?" He offered me his hand.

I smiled and shook it. He must've held my hand too long because Evan pulled me back to walk in the other direction. I was so embarrassed. Rashaad was nothing but kind and respectful. My man acted like some controlling asshole.

Evan took my hand and led us deeper into the club. I yanked away from his grip. He whipped around with a furrowed brow. We stared at each other for a few moments.

My heart sped up and a slap played out in my thoughts. Talking myself out of making a scene, I turned and headed for the exit. I slid through tight spots that his tall ass couldn't get through. I wanted to lose him to get a second alone.

I made it outside, stomping the whole time. When he grabbed my hand, I pulled away hard. "Kay? You a'ight?" Rashaad asked.

"I'm sorry. I thought you were my man."

"Everything good with y'all?"

"Before what he just did, yes. He's tripping right now."

"He doesn't hurt you or nothing, right?"

"Oh, hell no! Evan's not like that. It's a long story. I'm not in danger or anything."

"Don't lie. We may not have been in touch, but I'll fuck a nigga up if he put his hands on you."

I smiled before laughing. Rashaad's bearded face hid those dimples I used to love. "Evan is a good guy. Thank you for caring. Besides, I would never put up with that shit."

"You better not. It wouldn't be the first time I had to fight for you." We cracked up at the thought of a little brawl in our school's hallway because of this guy who kept bothering me. Rashaad was just as protective back then.

"Babe?" His voice came from behind Rashaad. I rolled my eyes.

"Evan, don't start."

He stood next to me. "Look, I'm sorry."

Rashaad's suspicion took over his face. I knew it looked terrible. "We're good. I promise. We'll catch up soon," I told him.

Evan's face tightened. I waited to see if he'd jump stupid, but he didn't.

"A'ight, girl. Ay, it was nice meeting you, Evan. You got a good one on your hands. Treat her right."

"I do."

Rashaad sized Evan up before slowly walking away.

"Let's go. I'm ready to go." I put some distance between us.

"Kim, what's wrong? I said sorry."

"I heard you. Let's go."

Back in our room, I kept my silence. Evan had to understand that a man could speak to me without it being anything more than a friendly conversation.

"You really mad at me?" he asked. I glared at him with no answer.

The only thing that would get my attention was a long, hot shower. Ignoring him while gathering what I needed, he grabbed me. One hard push on his chest confirmed my irritation and he backed off. Evan tried to come into the bathroom minutes later, but I locked the door.

When I finished and came out, he stood from the bed. "Kim, talk to me."

"Are you sure? Because it seems like you have a problem with me talking to men. I don't want to risk you getting pissed at yourself."

He sucked his teeth. "Come on, babe. I thought he hit on you."

"Well, I'm flattered that you assume every man wants me. News flash, they don't."

"Oh, please. I watched the both of you first. You touched him too, and he drooled when you did. What the hell was I supposed to think?"

"That you can trust me. I'm not that type of woman. Never have been." His head titled. "And if you bring up Brian, I will fucking slap you."

"Baby, calm down. I'm sorry. It looked like something else from where I stood. Like you were flirting with some random dude. All that touching shit ain't cool."

I raised my brow at his tone. "I barely touched him. He did not touch me besides a damn hug."

"Whatever, Kim. You don't understand."

"No, you don't understand. I am not your ex-wife! I can be around dudes without fucking them."

"Wow. That's what we're doing?"

"You started it. Being rude as hell. He asked if you were abusive. You can't act like that with me. You have to trust me."

"Okay, Kim. It's all on me. You did nothing wrong. It's never your fault." His sarcastic tone sounded too damn familiar.

Those words slapped me in the face. Trent used to say the same thing.

I put my clothes away and walked to the balcony when I felt tears coming. I sat in a chair and let the cool breeze calm my nerves.

Evan gave me about ten minutes of peace before he interrupted it, joining me outside. He sat too close and noticed my puffy eyes. "Kim, why are you crying? It's okay. I'm not tripping over that dude. It was stupid of me to think you'd disrespect what we have. I know better. You don't have to cry. I didn't mean to upset you."

He held me, and I rested my head on his chest. "I'm not mad. I see how it could've looked to you. I'm sorry for being careless."

"It's okay. Really it is. My bad for not trusting you."

We kissed and tears fell again. I wiped them away. "Sorry. They keep coming."

"Talk to me. What's making you cry? We can fix it. I hate seeing you like this, babe."

"You said something Trent always threw in my face, and I never considered it to be true. For you to say it means that it was."

I explained to Evan the problems Trent and I always had. Even though much of the time Trent was at fault, I realized that my actions weren't always innocent. In this relationship, I needed accountability. No repeats of the same crap because of my own blindness to my faults.

Evan apologized for taking me back to my old relationship. He swore up and down he didn't mean what he said. He did, and he was right, but I didn't argue with him about it.

We spent the last day on the beach and discussed our past in detail. For hours we learned things about each other that explained so much. Evan had been cheated on more than once which made him jealous when he didn't need to be. I assumed his trust issues only stemmed from his ex-wife.

It was crazy how much we didn't know over the year together. Learning about what he'd gone through in relationships and the admiration for his parents' marriage made me love him more. I understood his pain and never wanted to contribute to it.

Our reservations for the night came up quick. I asked him to cancel. I wanted to chill for our last night. It disappointed him, claiming the restaurant was supposed to be the highlight of our trip. I convinced Evan that being with him alone on our balcony meant more than some fancy restaurant. I eventually got my way.

Back home, I asked for a couple of weeks to get myself together. Evan and I needed space. All this time up under each other did something to me.

We texted throughout our short break but not an annoying amount. He only checked on me. At first he took it wrong and assumed the worst. After promising him that this wasn't the end of us, he relaxed.

Evan admitted that the break did some good. He told me it put things in perspective for him about our relationship. All of his doubts left his thoughts. I felt the same way. A future with him was what I wanted. I loved him.

CHAPTER NINETEEN

Today, everything was finally going according to plan. I attempted to pull this off twice since our anniversary. Each time something got in the way. Nothing would stop me now. Not my past. Not Kim's. Not even my mother's understandable concerns.

I paced the floor as the call came in that Kim was on her way to the house. I asked the security at the gate to tell us when she arrived. Vivica, Tara, Marissa, and I scrambled around for the last two hours getting everything in order. Good thing they agreed to give me a hand.

The most exciting part was using Ava to help me pull this off. Plus, the ladies would join in on my performance soon. The beautifully dressed angel took my hand when I reached for her and we walked closer to the front door to wait on her mother.

Kim had a hair and nail appointment as she regularly did. She'd get up early on a Saturday morning and head out for her beauty routine. This time she'd come home to a surprise.

My heart sped up when I heard her pull into the driveway.

Whether from nerves or the suit, I perspired. The ladies stood in the kitchen awaiting Kim's entrance. I picked Ava up so she wouldn't run to her mom. We rehearsed something special which required her to stay next to me.

It was only the early afternoon, so all the lights were out in the living room and kitchen so that the dozens of lit candles illuminated the room. With the shades halfway down on the back windows, the place exuded romance. Rose petals were everywhere. I promised Vivica I'd sweep it all up myself.

There she was. Kim opened the front door slowly, then stopped once she saw part of the setup. Her eyebrows grew closer. "Uh, what is going on?"

"Come in and find out." To my surprise, Ava didn't try to jump down. Her little arm was around the back of my neck, and her head rested near my ear.

Kim gasped when she walked all the way inside and let the door shut behind her. "Evan, what are you...What is this?"

I made my way closer and her eyes already watered. "You will see." I nodded at Tara, cueing her to start the music.

Jagged Edge's "I Gotta Be" played in the background as I led Kim to the first stop. It was a small, but tall stand with a picture of the two of us. Tea lights surrounded it for a soft glow.

"Remember this?" I asked.

She nodded. "Yeah. It was the first time we went out."

"Do you remember what I said to you that night?"

Her body froze briefly, more tears dropped. "That you hoped it was your last first date," she barely got out.

I kissed her and Ava touched her mother's face, then she handed Kim the handkerchief I'd just given her.

After wiping her eyes, I led Kim to an identical setup with a different picture. "What about this one?"

Still patting her eyes, she looked up at me. "Our three-month anniversary. You insisted that we take Ava to dinner with us. She hated the food."

We laughed, including the ladies standing by in the kitchen. "We should've taken her to a more kid-friendly restaurant. I learned that lesson quick."

"Evan?" she said, grabbing my free hand. "Are you sure you want to do this?"

"Shhh." I refused to allow her fears to stop what was inevitable. My lifelong goal was to make her understand that she deserved to be happy. We both did. I kissed her hand. "Let's go to the next one."

Once she saw it, she groaned. "Ugh! Why do you have that picture?"

"To remind you I will always take care of you. Even when you are as sick as a dog."

"Aww, babe!" I got a kiss for that one. "But that is an ugly picture."

"You look beautiful as always."

"Can't Take My Eyes Off of You" by Lauryn Hill played next.

"I had tissue stuffed in my nose. My mouth is all open," Kim complained.

"Yep, still beautiful."

Lauryn's vocals took Kim's attention, and we sang part of the song together. She really got into it.

The next stand held a picture when we visited Houston. Kim's face soured at the sight. Not really at the photo itself. We took a selfie at the airport in front of the Houston graffiti mural above the stairs leading to baggage claim.

"That was a horrible trip, babe."

"I know, but I want you to know that I will love you through anything. Nothing will ever change that. We aren't our past, and I learned then to only see the woman I fell in love with. Not the things that make you feel unworthy of that love."

More tears fell from Kim's already swollen eyes. "You are too good to me. How did I get so lucky?"

"No, I'm the lucky one." We walked to the second to last table where a collage of Kim, Ava, and me sat. "Even though this little one does not share my DNA, I love you both as my family. I would die for her and do everything in my power to protect you two and provide all that you both need."

"I love you," Kim whispered.

"Love you, too." I kissed her lips again.

I glanced up at the ladies watching us. They were all crying. I guess that meant it was going well. I gave Tara another nod to play the instrumental song. I switched Ava to my other side and took Kim's hand.

Once the music started, her eyes lit up before tearing up. I pulled her close and sang John Legend's "Stay With You." My background singers did their best through their tears. It was perfect.

My baby cried more every time she looked up at me. The three of us danced throughout the song. Kim loved my voice more than I did, so I had to sing to her on this special occasion.

When we finished, my DJ played the final song. Kim's favorite one. Another ballad by Jagged Edge. "The Rest of Our Lives."

The intro to that one made her close her eyes and bring her hands to her chest. "Evan."

"Okay, angel. It's time," I told Ava.

I put her down and held her hand as she grabbed Kim's. The three of us walked to the dining table with rose petals and large candles everywhere. This one had an empty picture frame. Confusion spread across Kim's face. "What's this one supposed to be?"

"Our future. A clean slate. Open to infinite possibilities."

I got on one knee and sat Ava on it. After finally pulling the box out of my pocket, I opened it with Ava's help. Kim's cries grew louder, but the song still played which meant I didn't miss the end. That was her favorite part.

"I already have Ava's approval. We discussed it thoroughly." She laughed. "I even received your father's blessing. So, the only person left to ask is you. Kimberly Chanel Duncan, will you marry me?"

"Yes! Yes!" she said with no hesitation. The ladies squealed and clapped.

Grabbing Kim's left hand, I slid the ring onto her ring finger. Vivica told me what she assumed was Kim's ring size. She was right. The three-carat princess cut diamond ring fit perfectly. My gorgeous lady gazed at her hand with her mouth ajar.

I stood up holding Ava and kissed my fiancée for the first time. This one was longer than the others. Once we pulled away, Vivica had already taken the champagne from the refrigerator.

All the women hugged her and checked out the ring. Vivica wouldn't let me show them until after Kim accepted. She thought it was bad luck. Never heard that one before, but I went with it in case it held any weight. It didn't matter now. She said yes.

One year was not very long, but the things we'd overcome in that short period led me to believe we could do anything together. Especially this hard obstacle called life.

Our mothers would eventually come around. I hoped. Whether they did or not never mattered. I knew I wanted to marry Kim the second I laid eyes on her. That realization gave me the balls to ask her out during Ava's appointment.

We'd grown into a family already, and I wanted to add siblings for Ava from her mother. I understood that Kim didn't have things in the order she dreamed they'd happen, but I would work my ass off to make sure it was worth the wait.

After handing Ava to her mom, I popped open the bottle. Kim still wiped her eyes repeatedly as she picked up one of the champagne flutes from the counter. I filled all of our glasses.

Vivica got our attention and volunteered to make a toast. I was relieved because I didn't consider a speech. It took a lot to plan what I'd say for each picture.

"You's getting married now!" Vivica said. We all chuckled at somewhat *The Color Purple* imitation.

Vivica cleared her throat. "In all seriousness, you are like my daughter and I remember when you first came here. You were lost in the mess you thought would be the rest of your life. Then Ava entered the world and put a joy in your eyes that had never been there before. I always believed you deserved all the happiness that could come your way.

"You got discouraged from the things and people you could not change, and I prayed for a miracle to change your world and your perception. Never did I think God would package it in a tall, dark, and fine brother whose job was to make sure your daughter stayed healthy. You were so fine yourself, the man couldn't even do his job."

We laughed out loud at that one. It was true. Kim kissed me again with more love than ever.

"Look at the two of you now. Drama thought it could consume any ounce of happiness that tried to enter your life and you told it to 'go to hell.' And you, Evan, are a good man if I'd ever seen one. The only good ones I thought existed were my late husband, my sons, and my brother."

"Yeah, that's because you think it had something to do with you," Kim remarked.

Her aunt narrowed her eyes at her. "You lucky Evan just promised to protect you."

Kim looked at me. "Yes, he did. That includes from you."

"Hey, don't get me into trouble," I said. We all laughed.

"I am so proud of the way you both held on to each other through situations that would have separated the weak. You two are far from weak, which is why I know deep down in my soul you will be together forever. God bless your soon-to-be union and may He bless you two to be fruitful. I could use about six more little ones running around when the family comes over."

"Nope! You better throw that prayer at Tara and Marissa. We will definitely have kids, but you ain't getting that many from my body."

I agreed in silence.

Ava had gotten bored with my plans to become a more significant part of her life. She'd fallen asleep on Kim's shoulder. I picked her up and took her to her room. When I removed her shoes, I pulled her blanket over her only leaving her head uncovered.

I kissed her on the cheek and stared at this beautiful little girl that will soon be my stepdaughter. I already loved her as such. Then her future sisters or brothers crossed my mind as I stood next to her bed. Too much time must have passed because Kim walked into the room looking for me.

"Are you okay, Ev?"

"Yeah, I was thinking about our future kids."

"Well, maybe we need to get on making a baby right after the wedding. Ava's only two, and it will be good for her to have siblings not too much younger than her."

"Shoot, we can practice tonight," I said kissing her neck.

"Mmm, we should. You know, to make sure we'd do it right." Kim turned to face me before kissing my lips. "Aunt Vivica can babysit. We need to celebrate alone."

"Indeed! I love you, soon-to-be Mrs. Kimberly Thomas."

"Mmm, I like the sound of that."

"I'm ready to get out of here so I can hear some of my favorite sounds from you." I poked her with my growing erection.

"You so nasty. I love you too, Mr. Thomas."

CHAPTER
TWENTY

I RUSHED OVER TO MY MOM'S HOUSE AFTER SHE TOLD me there was an emergency. Denise's car was outside.

"What is it? What happened?" I spat out as soon as I walked in.

Denise's face was wet from crying. Mom stood from holding her and walked toward me. "Mom, what's going on? What happened?"

"Her grandmother passed away last night. They found her unresponsive in her bed this morning."

Damn. I quickly took over consoling my wife. When I held her in my arms, she cried more. I didn't know what to say, so I stayed quiet. Mom told me Layla was napping in the back.

"What can I do?"

"Nothing. She's gone. We can't do anything." Denise's voice trembled. "She died in her sleep. She's really gone. I should've stayed there."

Who could've known she'd pass away so suddenly? After she beat the illness that had a better chance of taking her life, everyone assumed she had a lot more time.

Her grandmother just visited us for Thanksgiving. She seemed perfectly healthy for her age.

"I need to go lay down."

"Okay, baby. You can take the guest room. I put Layla down on my bed. Take all the time you need. Brian and I will call your parents soon."

Denise nodded and got up. On her way to the room, she darted toward the bathroom. We heard her throw up. I hopped up from the couch, but my mom made me stop from checking on her. "She's okay. This happens. She's fine."

Mom and I walked to the backyard to sit and talk. She told me that Denise was dropping Layla off and got the call when she arrived. They'd been here for more than an hour before Mom told me to come over. I felt helpless.

ppp

THE FOLLOWING WEEKEND, all of us flew to Atlanta together for the funeral. The service had me in tears. My wife spoke about her grandmother's impact on her life, and she could barely get the words out. I hated seeing her in so much pain.

That night, after everyone left her parents' house, we all sat around the living room and kitchen area. Aunt Rita couldn't stop mentioning her excitement of our reconciliation. Bam informed me that I was one more slip-up away from going missing. Mom got on her about threatening me with some threats of her own.

The next morning, Denise woke up sick again. Whenever I pried about her wellbeing, she'd let me know that stress caused nausea lately. She went through the same sickness after we separated. I didn't remember her doing it in the past, then again, she never had so many stressful situations either.

After breakfast, Mom and Patti snickered like children. I

loved seeing them together because it meant that we were all family still. Stan and I took Layla out to the park to give Denise some space. She really took the passing of her grandmother hard, and since it was so fresh, I didn't want to crowd her by trying to comfort her 24/7.

When we got back, all three ladies sat in the living room talking. Stan grabbed beers for us and offered the women some wine. Denise declined because she already had a drink. Her eyes were fresh from tears.

"So, Brian, how's life been now that you have your family back?" Patti asked.

"Better than I imagined. I mean, we don't live together or anything." Denise asked for a week to consider the move a month ago. "She renewed her lease, so I have a lot more work to do. We're getting there, right?" I glanced at my wife. She nodded and took a drink of whatever was in her cup.

"There are ways around that. You guys need to be under the same roof more than ever now." Mom smiled at me.

"We can take as much time as she needs. I'm okay with that."

Patti glanced Denise's direction. "When is the new lease up?"

"Six months," Denise answered, but barely opened her mouth to say it.

"Oh, that will not do. Y'all need to get yourselves together now. Life is too short. What's the holdup? We understand you two have been doing *very* well."

Denise brought her hand to her forehead. "Really, Momma?"

"What? You have, haven't you? Anyone in your condition must have been doing something right." She smiled at her daughter the same way my mom did.

Mom winked at me still smiling too hard. "Did I miss something?"

"Son, you're just meant to be slow, aren't you? He doesn't get that from my side of the family. I tell you that." Our mothers laughed.

I looked at Stan, and he shrugged as if he wasn't in on the joke. Denise got up and grabbed my hand. "I need to talk to you outside."

"Okay." I followed her lead, and we sat on the rocking bench.

"So, what's going on with the women in this house today? They are being weird as hell."

"Our family is crazy. That's nothing new. Momma is just happy that we are working everything out."

"Yeah, that makes sense. She was definitely rooting for us."

Denise cleared her throat. "So...I've been sick for a minute."

"Stress, right?"

"You can say that, but it started before I found out about Nana."

"What are you saying? Is something wrong? Like health wise?"

"Yes, and no."

"Babe, tell me what's going on. What is it?"

"I...well, we, um..."

I faced her. "Dee?"

"I'm pregnant, Brian."

"P-Pregnant? You're...what?"

"Yeah. It looks like we're having another baby."

The first thing that came to mind was how. We didn't use protection, but it never occurred to me that I'd get her pregnant. If anything, I assumed she was taking birth control or something.

"How do you feel about it?"

"Brian, I really don't know. It's not like it matters since it's already done."

"It matters. Are you mad? Happy?"

"On the one hand, Layla gets to be a big sister. On the other hand, we aren't together, together."

"I can't believe it. How far along?"

"Not sure. I took the test, well more like four tests, a couple weeks ago. I haven't seen a doctor yet. I guess I was in denial, but with all the symptoms and the positive tests, I wasn't in a rush to officially confirm it."

"So, that's what they're up to in there."

Denise nodded. "After the first test, I called my momma crying hysterically. She was so excited, and I was pissed at her for being happy about it. I told Nana too. I got the call that she passed away right after I told your mom. That's why I was really at her house that day."

"I'm the last to know?"

"Pretty much." She giggled. "What do you think about it?"

"Honestly, I want you to move in right now. What are we waiting for? We're about to have a baby." I stood up. "Damn, we are really having another baby!" I pulled Denise from her seat and held her. I couldn't stop my tears. I tried to suck it up, but the thought of us being a real family again got to me. She leaned back when she heard me sniffle. Then she started up. I didn't need her crying too.

The worst time in my life was behind me. My wife, my babies, and I had so much life ahead of us.

"So, does this mean you will break your lease? You've been taking a long ass week."

Denise laughed so hard, she snorted. "God must be on your side because I was going to wait it out then decide."

"Yeah, He gotta be. I've screwed up so bad, I knew my life was over. By His grace, I got another chance. I will not let Him nor my family down. I learned my lesson the hard way. I don't understand why God blessed me with you even after I proved

I'm not worthy. I won't question His gift. You're finally coming home."

"There's no point in living apart anymore."

"Will I really have to sleep in my office?" She burst out laughing.

"I'm just saying. It's not like we ain't...I mean the proof is inside you."

Denise rolled her eyes. "We can share the same room, Brian."

"Oh, thank God. I did not want to have to sleep on the futon every night. I would've, but damn I didn't want to."

"Silly."

"I love you." I lowered my head to her belly. "I love you too son or daughter." I kissed her there.

"I love you, too. Let's do this for real this time. No more dumb shit."

"I promise you, no more dumb shit." I kissed my pregnant wife before we returned to meet our grinning parents.

"Congratulations!" our moms shouted.

"Thank you." I couldn't believe Mom kept it to herself. All those silly faces and goofy smiles made sense now.

Patti stood up and gave me the biggest hug. "I'm so proud of you. You keep her happy, you understand me?" she whispered in my ear.

"Yes, ma'am."

She released me and nudged me in the chest. "I'm getting another grandbaby!"

Stan hugged his daughter. "Well, we are greatly outnumbered. Denise, I'm gon' need you to focus on boys all day, every day, so that baby will get the hint."

We all laughed. "It doesn't work like that, Dad. But okay."

"It's still time. You aren't too far along according to your momma. So, boy thoughts."

"Yeah, sure." Denise made circles around the side of her ears.

Patti walked to the kitchen and came back with another beer for me. "Oh, baby, tell them the good news."

Stan looked confused at first. "Yeah, yeah! So, we're moving back to Houston."

Denise gasped and put on a wide grin.

Her dad continued. "We were only here for Nana, and since she's with the Lord, we have no reason to stay."

"Well, what about the house?" Denise asked.

"Rita will move in and take care of the place. This house is paid for, and we will never sell it. This is where we grew up. There are too many memories. My daddy worked too hard to pay for this house for us to not keep it in the family," Patti explained.

"That's great! We will need all the support we can get back home with two kids." I pat my father-in-law on the shoulder.

Mom raised her glass of wine. "This is for never giving up on each other and never giving up on love."

"Here, here." Patti tapped her glass against my mom's. I did the same with Stan and then the ladies.

I turned to my wife. "To the rest of our lives."

"To the rest of our lives."

CHAPTER
TWENTY-ONE

Denise

Brian set the box on the floor. "That's everything. I'll go with my mom to return the moving truck."

"Good. I will take Layla back to the apartment and make sure it's clean. I'll drop off the keys and head back here."

Brian hugged me, then picked me up. "I love you."

"I love you too."

"This is real. You are really here with me."

"Unless you think you will do something else to make me leave again."

"Hell, naw. Never will I ever be so stupid."

"I hope not."

Brian kissed my lips hard as hell. "Never."

Debbie and Layla walked through the front door. Her wide smile had to hurt. "Oh, are we interrupting anything?"

After another kiss, Brian put me down. "No. You ready to go? I know you just walked in."

"Yeah, I'm ready." Debbie released Layla's hand, and my baby walked to us. Brian lifted her up, and we both gave her a kiss. She always got a good laugh at double-teamed kisses.

"We'll be back soon. I'll get you some bread pudding on the way."

"Ooh, you are going for major brownie points today, huh?"

"Something like that." Brian licked his bottom lip with that look in his eyes.

Debbie smacked her lips. "Boy, come on. Y'all have forever to make up with your nasty selves."

He laughed. "Sorry, Mom."

We left the house together.

The apartment was in great shape. I didn't have to do much at all. After one last walk-through, I dropped off the keys and drove back home.

After all that we'd gone through in this house, it meant so much to call it home again. Layla now lived with both parents like she should've always been privileged to do. She'd have what she deserved.

Later that evening, we put away most of my things. There wasn't much between the two of us. Brian already moved the extra furniture in storage. We'd sell most of it soon enough.

Debbie stayed over most of the day, helping us out with Layla while we got the house together. She left after my bug fell asleep. I loved that woman. Without her and my parents, Brian and I would not be back under the same roof.

Last month she had to jump in the middle of a disagreement between Brian and me. I got upset about him talking to Kim in my presence. Something about the length of their conversation and the fact that it wasn't all about the baby pissed me off. I remember him congratulating her on getting engaged and wondered why the hell she called to tell him.

Debbie told me about Kim and Brian discussing her moving back to Houston so he could see Ava more. Even though Kim mentioned to Debbie that she didn't feel comfortable moving back for whatever reason previously, her engagement would keep her in California. She only told Brian to tell him she was staying permanently.

I still had a problem with their communication because they talked about me. Brian once asked about the emails Kim sent. I got them and as soon as I saw her name, I deleted each one. I even flagged them as spam. I didn't care what she had to say then and still didn't.

Another thing I didn't understand nor appreciate was why they spoke so often and how Brian went to a different room to talk with her. Debbie also explained the same things that Brian did. Those conversations usually ended with video chats with Ava. He only left the room to be respectful and kept me away from it all.

Agreeing to start over with Brian meant being aware of his other relationships. He was a parent with Kim and nothing I felt would change it. I had to accept that they had to communicate to be good parents.

It would take me some time to be okay with it since I lived with him. But damn it was hard. I wished we could be done with Kim and that part of our lives. However, Brian was set on being a good father, and I could no longer fault him for that.

We called it a night after the long day of moving and unpacking. Brian ran me a bubble bath with my tablet sitting on the window seat. Netflix was on the screen waiting for me to pick something to watch while I relaxed. He even filled my favorite tumbler with ice water in case I got too hot.

After a half hour in the tub, I got out ready to sleep for days. I turned the TV on when I sat on my side of the bed. Brian was lying on his side reading something on his phone.

"So, what do you want to do for our first official night back together?"

"You are so corny. We don't have to do anything. All I really want to do is sleep. Your child is wearing me out already." He kissed my stomach.

"I still can't believe we created another life."

I rolled my eyes. "You probably did it on purpose to get me to stay."

"Yeah right. I can't make you do nothing you don't want to."

"True. You still knocked me up on purpose."

"The only thing I did was make love to my wife. Sometimes the result is a baby. I didn't hear you complaining when we were making him or her."

"Shut up."

I laid back on my pillow trying to get comfortable. Something poked me through it. I moved the pillow ready to find one of Layla's toys that always appeared in odd places. A small red box sat there. Brian couldn't hold back his smile.

"Boy, what is this?"

"What is that?" He shrugged his shoulders too hard.

"You are such a bad actor." I opened the box and found a sparkling wedding ring with three diamonds across it and a band with diamonds lined around it. "Brian?"

He had already made it to my side of the bed and knelt down. "Dee, I know this was a tough time for us, and I can't thank God enough that you are here with me. Wherever your original ring is, I don't care. We missed a couple anniversaries, so you needed this upgrade anyway. This time, I swear to honor what this ring represents.

"You and I were meant for each other. What we've overcome is our proof. So with this ring, I promise to love and protect you. I promise to be your provider, your lover, and your best friend. I never want to be apart from you again. I want you forever."

My lips quivered as the tears blocked my sight of him. When I wiped my face, I noticed that he was crying. "Dee, I want to do it right this time with no setbacks. Will you accept this ring?"

"As long as my soon-to-be fat ass doesn't have to squeeze into a wedding dress, of course, I will."

He kissed me and took the rings from the box and placed them on my finger. "Whatever you want. We can have another wedding or a small ceremony with you, me, and Layla. Or even nothing at all if you don't want to. I wanted you to have this new commitment from me since I destroyed the last one."

"I understand, babe. I would love to have a small ceremony. We can do it with our parents and the pastor. They're supposed to be here in two or three months. Their house should be ready by then."

"Perfect." He got up from the floor and pushed me back on my pillow.

While on top of me, he kissed my neck a few times. "I guess it's too late to try for twins."

"You are too silly. We can try." I bit his lip.

He burst out laughing. "Look at you!" With a quick roll, Brian pulled me on top of him. "Let's get to it then."

I kissed his lips. "I love you."

"I love you, Dee. More than you'll ever know. I damn sure will prove it forever."

"You'd better."

The End.

AFTERWORD

Straightaway means no more turns. In these characters' cases, no more dumb shit (as Denise said).

Turns in Love was my exploration of loving two people and still being happy with the person you chose. You've read how these people made so many wrong turns but eventually got on the right road.

I really hope that you enjoyed these couples. Kim has come a long was on her own. After being the cause of so much pain, she had to learn how to forgive herself and realize that she was still worthy of love and happiness. If God can forgive our major screw ups, we should too.

Denise's struggle was many women's struggle. Forgiving someone who hurt her. Brian may have not deserved it but grace works like that. I needed her to find her way to that point. As a reminder to us all that even if we don't go back into a relationship, grace is needed to forgive and move on.

This series was fun yet difficult. I hate putting my characters in these situations. However, it's always rewarding to find out how they maneuver through what I throw at them.

Please leave a review of Turns in Love. I'd love to hear (read) your thoughts.

ABOUT THE AUTHOR

Renée is from Houston but lives in Minnesota with her husband and kids. She writes fiction based on African American characters. Renée loves creating stories with relationship drama that can easily be found in many households. She wants readers to see themselves or recognize someone they know in her characters. If she can make you laugh, gasp, think, or even cry, then her mission will be accomplished.

Connect with Renée: www.authorramoses.com www.facebook.com/authorramoses On Instagram @reneeamoses

Listen to Same Book, 3 Time Zones: A Book Review Podcast
www.sb3tzreviews.com
On Instagram @sb3tz_reviews

For a FREE copy of Almighty Judge Diana Duncan short backstory
bit.ly/TILShort
Or a FREE copy of Truth Is
bit.ly/TruthIsFC

Signup for latest news, updates, and exclusive content:
www.authorramoses.com/signup

ALSO BY RENÉE A. MOSES

Turns in Love Series

Two Lefts, One Right

Making a Hard Right

Straightaway*

Wishing for Her

Truth Is...

Harris Sisters Series

The Cost of Loving You

I Thought I Knew You

Never Stopped Loving You

Not Good Enough For You

Standalone

You Could Do Damage

When the Time is Wright (Christmas Novella)